The Books and the Sea

A collection of short stories

Jane Coutts

Acknowledgements

As with my first book, I cannot sufficiently thank my friend Yvonne McHugh for her patience, suggestions and encouragement in making these stories a reality. Thanks also to my husband, not only for creating the book's cover, but also for his faith in me and not least for his own stories, which all too few people have taken the time to listen to. Thanks, as ever, to my mother and father, because – probably against everyone's advice – they have allowed me to take a path less trodden. My sister and brother-in-law deserve special thanks for always being at the end of a phone to help me through the more conventional of life's obstacles. Thanks of a less tangible nature go to all the people who indirectly – and unwittingly – inspired the characters in these tales: my teachers, my (and my husband's) wayward ancestors, my mother-in-law and a man who loved birds for their own sake. Finally, many, many thanks to all the books on my shelves, and on everyone's shelves, and to the booksellers who take care of the ones which have been forgotten.

For more information about this book, visit:
http://www.booksandthesea.com/

Also by this author – Merinder's House:
http://www.merindershouse.com/

To my sons, Temmy and Frank, in the hope that they never quite lose the stories we have given them, no matter what happens and no matter who tries to persuade them otherwise.

The Three Knots

Losing My Father

Many, many years ago, when people were still afraid of the sea, and did not taunt it and call it by its name, my father went away to work. He left us with the women to watch over a house he rarely lived in, but for which he was to some degree responsible. He was probably glad to be away, because I am told my father was a man who could not bear to listen to the daily ills of the small world, and could find nothing fair about them. Like all the others who went away, he took a boat to the town and reported to any ship he had heard of which might need crew.

Had my father ever been forced to live with us all the time, he would have run away anyway. Most of the men who went to sea said they went because they had to, because there were too many mouths to feed at home, but I knew that was not true. Most of them only lived because they could leave, and coming home was something they occasionally thought they wanted.

Sometimes my father went to places where the sun shone, and sometimes to places like ours, where it hid, and turned pale men red when it finally appeared. Sometimes, on his fleeting visits home, he brought us strange things, which we could not eat and which baffled my mother, like teacups made of thin china that shone like shells, and glass beads which rolled along the table.

Sometimes he went to places to kill whales, and he brought us animals made from whalebone and walrus tusks, which he said were made by men who had walked on ice. Sometimes he went to places where people lived in houses on sticks, and where wild pigs ran like fury through something he called a forest, but which sounded more like a jungle. In those days I did not know the difference, but I learned words the other children did not, whose fathers stayed at home and drew their world around themselves.

And that was sometimes a problem because children are stronger whose fathers are there to defend them, and I was on the wrong end of many a speculation from boys who had their fathers at home. Their fathers' secrets were of the kind not to be spoken of, but of a sordid nature, while my father, who was not there and whose transgressions were unknown, could be speculated upon with impunity.

I had learned not to speak about my father in public, nor to draw attention to his absence, because this is how a boy survives in a small world which he does not understand and where people have a need to be better than others. I barely remembered what he looked like, because in the photographs he always appeared hidden behind other men, and he made excuses about getting his portrait taken to send home like the others.

He was invariably away for a long time, or so it seemed, and I knew when he had sent us money because my mother took us all to the merchant to stock up with flour and, if I was lucky, sugar. I was seven. Not old enough to be responsible and not young enough to be carefree, and I helped when I was told to. When the helping was done, I went down to my aunt, who lived by the beach.

I went to her house in the afternoons before tea, and hoped she would not have visitors. I liked being with her in her house, because I was a strange child, who did not seek the company of other children. I asked my aunt questions, trying to provoke a smile or a long answer or both, and hoped she would become interested enough in my questioning to sit down with me in the fading light, and tell me about something more than I had asked for.

One day, I asked her why she had never married, and she said it was because she was in love with what she could not have, and served her brothers who needed her to help them when they came home from sea or when their wives died which, for some reason, they often did. "And also," she added, looking down at me over her round spectacles, "to mind their wayward children."

But she also knew I was not wayward, and only spent time in her house because there was no room in mine. My brothers were older and more useful, and it was better if I was out from under their feet. So I went down to my aunt's house by the beach, and sat with her in the afternoons, to keep her company and to ask her about the world.

I always walked down the narrow path between the two stone walls, because otherwise the men in the fields would see me and ask me to help them with their work. I was bored by the fields, and the men intimidated me with their jokes. They had forgotten their childhoods and no longer remembered what it felt like to have to dodge in and out of grown men's frivolity, trying not to become the butt of it.

My aunt's house, though, was safe in its dark corners. The house was small with two rooms, one where she slept, and one where she did everything else. If any of her brothers were home from sea, she slept on the straw bed in the clean end of the byre, and at times she went in there anyway and I had to wait patiently for her to come out. The byre was where she kept her secrets, such as they were.

Her house was unusually long compared to other people's houses, but smaller overall, like a narrow galley. A door led straight from the house to the byre where the cow lived, and the cow kept the house warm when the fire no longer could, for the island was rarely warm enough to heat our bones through. The house did not face the road, where people occasionally passed on their way to the merchant or to church, so to see who was coming, you had to go around to the blind side of the building and peer around the corner.

Instead, the house faced the sea. At times, it felt so close it might have threatened to come into the house itself, and my aunt was always sweeping sand across the threshold, back out onto the beach where it had come from. She said it was her penance for never having married, which was a more lenient explanation than I heard from the other boys.

My aunt was the only adult in the family who could read. All her brothers had been to the school given by the Minister, but they had had no aptitude or no interest, and struggled to hold a pencil in their thick fingers which preferred to haul ropes and carry cargo. My aunt, though, had found something in the words which helped her to live on, and when her brothers came home from sea, in return for her being there, they brought her books.

Because her brothers struggled to read, or to want to, they had little idea about the content of the literature they bought her, so her house and byre were filled with a library of such diversity that even the educated people in the town would have struggled to match its variety. There were books about correct manners and about railroads. Books on how to cook and about how to cure diseases with chemicals and liquid solutions. Books about kings and men of standing, and almanacs and numbers for calculating indeterminate things. There were verses and stories, a manual on how to lay the table for 100 guests, and even a timetable for sailings from a place called Bari.

Most curious of all, though, were the books about strange places, with images of smoking mountains and caves with dancing figures in reds and browns, and also the buildings in small towns with bowl-shaped roofs and slatted windows. There were paintings of beasts in deserts with stunted shadows where men were hiding. They were all but alive on the edge of the page.

Sometimes, the pictures were accompanied by verse and stories from these deserts and forests, and sometimes they were in strange languages, but that did not matter for the words danced just the same. Kalevala and Ibn Battuta, Gilgamesh and Ajdurai Mergen. Even now, during times when I do not know where to go in my head, when there is nowhere left to hide and I feel as though I am about to burst from the inside out, these names still come to me and play their music until I am able to sleep.

I learned to read at school, but I was not favoured by the teacher who had a thinly disguised dislike of my parents, and who therefore did her best to ensure I would grow up in ignorance. I was given to believe that I would amount to nothing, and so I acquiesced because it made life easier and I did not know the consequences.

This attitude filtered through to the playground, and whether it was because I was protecting myself from disappointment or because I really did not care, I did not push myself forward for the games the others played. As a consequence, I was not good at them, and when the older boys picked their teams, I was always last to be chosen, a reluctant hanger-on. My aunt's books and her quiet corners became a place where I would not have to make unnecessary choices. At times I only read the pictures, but they were the same, in a way, as the words. The colours and the sounds danced around in my mind until they merged.

My aunt worked hard, like everyone else, but she did not strain to add to the tedium of it, nor to do too much more than she needed, because she had other things to do. She was not one to follow the other women, nor to crave their company, which she had to endure often enough. They were a necessary social evil in a small world from which there was no escape.

But my aunt had her own secrets. My father once told me she should have been born a man, and she sometimes said that too. She meant, I think, that she could have gone away if she had been a man. On the other hand, she may never have found what she was looking for if she had, and she was just as likely to find it in her books. Unlike the other women, she did at least go somewhere to hide.

On occasions when she could not settle, she went into the byre and took out a piece of string from one of the wooden boxes. If the morning or afternoon sun had made an appearance, she would sit herself down on the step leading from the byre to the outside world, face the sea, and begin to tie knots. If I asked, she told me her brothers had taught her the knots, which they

15

had learned at sea when they tied ropes to hold down the cargo against the rolling of the waves and the storms they pitted themselves against. When she was in a good mood, though, and did not seem to have much else to do, she told me she tied the knots to hold down the storm and to speed my uncles home. She told me that if she untied the first knot, their boat would find a good breeze, and if she untied the second, it would be a fast wind and give them a speedy journey. Then always she was distracted, and something took her attention, and she got up to attend to whatever it was somewhere else.

My uncles were rarely all home at the same time. When one left, another arrived, but mostly they were not there at all because they were poor men who had to find a living in far-flung places where no-one else wanted to go, and because they could not stay. When they came back, they slept late and profited from the night, because they preferred the darkness for answering questions, as if the truth were less visible that way.

Sometimes they sat up and played cards all night, and this was when they came closest to one another, and to anyone who was with them around the table. Their sister always played cards with them, something the women only did when they were asked, but my aunt's participation had never been in question. She won her share, and lost her share, and laughed with the men. At these times, she was one of them and outside of herself.

My uncles sometimes arose from their long sleep while I was at the house, and when they emerged from their bed and found me there, huddled in a corner with my aunt's books, they were never quite sure how to speak to me. They were unused to children and considered them a territory to be approached with care, so they said little. They scratched their heads and found something to do in the house or the byre so that they would not have to look me in the eye. If any of them had whisky, though, rare in those days, or the one with the fiddle started to play, they came out of their shells, and sometimes relaxed in my presence as though the music brought impossible worlds together.

When her brothers left again, my aunt always gave them one of her pieces of string with its odd set of knots and told them to take care of it until the next time. They always took it, smiled, and put it in a pocket. I always assumed they never gave it another thought, and that the piece of rope stayed in their pocket until it fell out one day, or until they threw it away to make room for something else. I took their smile to mean they loved their sister and that they did not wish to hurt her feelings, because they knew they were the lucky ones, being able to get away.

One summer, there came a day when my mother arrived at my aunt's house while I was there, to say she had heard, via circuitous tongues, that my father might be coming home. Two of my uncles were already home, unusually at the same time, and her house was full. She had no space to move in her house, so she spent hours in the byre with her secrets.

My mother wanted to borrow flour until my father came home with money, so that she could have plenty of food when he came, and she would pay my aunt back later. My aunt was used to it and never got the flour back, but she equally needed her brother to be fed when he came home, and was grateful this brother's wife was still alive to take the work off her hands.

My father coming home broke the monotony and the lack of everyday things, but when I thought about it years later, the best feelings came with the anticipation of his return. When he arrived, so many people sought his attention, my mother, my older brothers, my aunt, that I had to find my place in the crowd, and do not remember it as well as the days before he arrived.

In those days, we woke up with hope, and with the thoughts of what he might bring with him, whether he would stay for a while or for no time at all. We wanted to think it would all be well, and for those few days it always was. There was no reason to think otherwise, and it would have been a waste of hope to be guarded and cautious. Only my aunt did not brim over with it all, and bided her time.

In such a mood of anticipation, my household began to get ready, and I was in the way. I went down to my aunt's house where it was safer to be a child. I found her in the byre with the door open towards the sea, and she was sitting with a piece of rope in her hands, tying or untying knots, I could not be sure which. She looked up when she saw me, and her hands fell limp in her lap. She turned away from me and looked out to sea, as though she could see my father approaching across the calm waters.

"Go in the house and fetch the box with my needles, there's a good lad."

I turned and went inside, aware in some vague way that something was not as it seemed. The box with her needles, some large and thick and others small with hardly a hole to thread through, sat on a small table by the fire, where she sat at nights if there was nothing more to do. I picked it up and took it to her, and she smiled as though it made everything all right.

She rummaged in the box for something, and said I could go in the house. She would be in shortly. I settled myself in the corner by the books I liked best, and opened one at a page with a picture of a tall mountain and a blue lake. For a long time, nothing came to disturb me, and I must have fallen asleep close to the warm fire.

When I woke up, my uncles were milling around the room, and my aunt was making soup and some fish they'd brought her from the rocky parts near the shore. Sometimes, that's what they did in the hours before the sun set. They went and sat by the sea, as if they hadn't had enough of it, and dragged a line back and forth until the odd passing fish bit the hook. Sometimes they waited for a long time and got nothing, but still they waited in the hours before the packs of cards came out.

My father was not a fisherman like his brothers. He and my aunt were the most alike, and had shared a pair of shoes when they were children. They went to church alternate Sundays, and he had ceded his place at the summer reading and writing so she could go every day, because otherwise she would only have learned the half and he would have learned nothing.

My father, instead, heard pictures in his head, mosaics of tiny pieces of coloured glass, musical notes which he could not write down with letters, but which he could draw with his long pencil and fill with yellow and blue ink when he could get it. Once he brought a small, rectangular block of black ink from China, with strange letters on it I did not recognise, and he told me to fetch him a cup of water from the well. Then he told me to sit down.

"Do you know what a mountain looks like?"

I had never seen a real one in our land of low hills, but I had seen them in my aunt's books. They were always white and had long sharp edges like frozen knives. My father said he liked to make mountains with the block of black ink, and I did not believe him because mountains did not look like that, but my father had seen more than I had, and I was not averse to his games so long as he stayed with me a while.

My father took a long piece of wood he called bamboo, which had at the end of it a hard brush which would not move. He dipped the tip of the brush in the cup of water I had brought him, and rubbed it slowly along the block he had set on the table. Then he put the brush back in the water. Finally, the brush touched the piece of paper he had in front of him, and he moved it furiously across the page. Then he looked at me, and saw the disappointment on my face. I had expected mountains and he had presented me with a piece of black paper.

"Watch," he said, pleased with my disbelief, and he added more water, and less water to the ink on the pen, until he had made reds and blues

22

and whites and blacks on the paper, and all over it were mountains and rivers and bridges and trees. The mountains hung over the rivers like gardens, and the trees had long tendrils like broken moss on the cliffs. Each time he dipped his brush into the water and floated it over the block of ink onto the page, the picture moved a little to its other side, and changed into something else.

When I asked him how he knew how to do it, he said someone had taught him in China, in a monastery by the sea where he had gone when the other crew were lost in the taverns. The man had told him how to hold the piece of bamboo so that it made a different colour each time it met the paper, depending on how hard he pressed it down and how much water he added. With the pen, the man had made letters and books, and pictures of trees that wept. He had been an artist and a man of precision, but a precision unlike any my father had known, which did not draw lines around itself.

Every time his ship docked in that port, he went to the man with the bamboo pens, and asked him the only questions he had asked of anyone as a grown man. That is how my father learned to put the pictures on paper that were in his head, even though none of his peers understood them and thought of it as some kind of party trick.

So now I was waiting for my father to come home so that he could paint me the mountains and the falling trees. Because my mother needed space in the house, I was allowed to stay late at my aunt's, and she made me a bed in the byre with some hay and a couple of wooden boards so that I did not need to go home if I fell asleep. It was the first time I had seen what happened when they all sat down to play cards.

They started late, and other men came down from the village, people who knew my uncles were home. Only at the cards did they speak freely and hear each other's news, and so they came down at night when all the women except my aunt had gone to bed. I sat in the corner, in trepidation at first, but later with interest, when I knew they did not give me a thought.

One of them dealt a hand, and there was silence for a few seconds while they contemplated their luck and guessed everyone else's. Then, while they played and each one laid down his cards, they talked and told stories about the men at sea and about the women in the ports. They laughed in between the hands and each had a new joke to tell, most of them not for my ears, but no-one cared and had forgotten I was there.

Not long into their game, something happened in the house which turned their heads. A wind rushed out of nowhere through the room and blew open the door, but there was no wind outside, only in the house. It was a wind that passed each of us, took its time and slid away again, so that my aunt looked up from her hand and her brow furrowed for a moment. My uncles looked at her, and at each other, because they knew her well, but the other men in the room said little and appeared not to have noticed the interruption. One of my uncles got up and closed the door, his cards still in his hand. My aunt motioned silently to him with a slight nod, and he returned to his seat so as not to draw anyone's attention.

They returned to their game, and after a while my aunt got up to stir some soup on the fire. Only then did she look perplexed, and fidgeted around the shelves in the semi-dark of the corners around the fireplace. She turned to her

25

brothers to ask if they had moved her spoon, which she needed to stir the soup, and they looked up distractedly from their hands and shook their heads.

It became clear to me, as the night wore on, that my father had not returned and that his brothers and sister did not seem overly concerned. They played on, and I must have fallen asleep because I woke up early in the morning on the straw mattress my aunt had made for me in the byre. She had already risen, and was outside clearing the sand. When she saw me awake, she told me my father had been delayed and that he might come that afternoon, so I could stay another night if I liked, to give my mother space.

My father did not come that time, nor did we hear from him for several more years. No-one knew where he was until one day, some years later, we heard from someone who had sailed with him to Greenland, and they said when they set off for home he was not with them, but no-one knew where he had gone. No-one had found a body, and there was still hope he was alive, maybe working on the Danish ships.

Not long after that, we got word that he was in the town and about to sail for the island. I was eleven, but still a child because I had not been forced away from the safety of this place like my brothers, and had no reason to doubt what I was told. On the other hand, I did not expect him to arrive, as he had not done so many other times before.

I was frustrated by my father's delay because, unlike the grown men, I had no measures to wait by, and did not know how much longer I would have to contain my excitement. I was fidgety, and went to my aunt who had no patience with my distraction, so she found me work to do. I swept the doorstep with its ubiquitous sand, and my eyes strayed out to sea, which was in its August state and calm. It billowed but did not roar, and the waves broke across the backbone of the beach with a certain grace.

By the afternoon, word came that my father's ship was due in that evening, if the weather held. I moped around the byre and then wandered out onto the beach a couple of times, wading through the eternity of an afternoon, and for some reason my thoughts turned to my aunt's pieces of rope with their thick knots. It occurred to me that, if my father's ship were about to have another delay, I might be able to hasten its passage, and I went back into the byre to look for one of the pieces of rope.

There were none in any of the wooden boxes my aunt kept there, just rusty metal hooks and pieces of iron hinges. I did not usually go near my aunt's things because she would not have taken kindly to it, but I began to snoop around her straw bed, and beneath it located a piece of her knotted rope. It was not smooth, as I had imagined, but rough and calloused, and its strands of hair pricked my hands as I stroked it against the grain.

It had three knots, and I prised the first one apart with a struggle, then wondered what to do with the rope. I put it back under the boards of my aunt's bed where I thought I had found it, but a thief rarely remembers the spot where he finds something as he generally does not intend to put it back. I returned to the house to await news of my father's arrival.

It was not unusual for ships to arrive several days after word came, and no-one was worried.

The summer weather did not invite concern. As my aunt came in to stoke the fire, though, she told me a breeze had blown up, and I needed to shut the door to keep the sand out otherwise I would have to sweep it all again.

I knew my father was not coming. I harboured brief fears that he might have found another ship, and heard the whales passing so that he had to follow. I half wondered if he had left me something in the town, to be delivered when someone was coming up, but I remembered the string in my aunt's byre and asked myself if the first knot had been too little, or had not given my father's boat enough speed.

I waited until my aunt was talking to her brother, who was home on a short stay, and then I slipped into the byre where the knots were. It was dark in there, and I had to feel my way, so that I did not know whether my aunt would notice I was not in the room. Guilty minds are more cautious than they need to be, but she did not see me leave, so I had little to fear.

I fumbled to find the string which I had hidden in haste, but eventually my fingers closed around it and I took the rope out again. I tugged at the last two knots, and when I opened the first one I fell back, such was the force it took out of me. I heard the door slam shut, but I was undeterred because I was at the age where boys cannot be told, and I did not even believe my own warnings. I prised open the third knot, and threw the rope carelessly back under the bed so I could get away fast, and there I waited, in the corner with the books.

A wind blew up so quickly no-one had seen it coming, and it was fiercer than any even my uncle said he had seen in all his years at sea. It tore away at the shoreline, and bounced stones against the door, which would not close until my uncle nailed a plank across it. Rocks the size of cannonballs were lobbed into the air and ripped through roofs of houses where they landed. People got out of their beds, but knew better than to be curious, or they would invite the storm. They huddled with furrowed brows against what was left of the embers, which swirled and threatened to blow around the room. At intervals, the wind exploded into the house, and through the window we could see the waves crashing close to the front door. They towered about the cliffs and whipped down onto the land, not just as spray like they usually did, but as walls of white water.

I looked at my aunt and she returned my gaze, though not until much later did she discover what it meant. Close to dawn the wind blew itself out. We all sat silently around the table, not even beginning to tidy up the debris outside because something more pressing was on our minds. My aunt did not have to tell me that the only hope for my father was that he had never left the town. We all hoped that this would be like all the other times he had never intended to come.

And they never knew, because they never heard from him again. They had come to know that this did not mean he was dead, but this time he never again sent word. We sometimes heard that someone had seen him, in some far away place where only sailors go, but they could never say for sure. I even saw him myself once or twice, such was my need to see him, though of course he was not really there.

I grew up after that night when my father did not come home. Quite suddenly I fought my way out of childhood and began to take on the duties of the household. It lasted until I went away, to wander the seas like my father, and to search for the man who drew coloured mountains with blocks of black ink. ∎

My Father - Greenland and Beyond

I am here now in this place after travelling for a long time. I find it pleasant enough, and want for very little as long as I can get up and keep walking. I have always been a restless soul, and could not settle with my children, nor with my wife, for all she was not a bad woman and for all I was not all good. I came here by chance, and only after a while did I understand what had happened. Most men would have been afraid of that, but I was relieved that I did not have to go back where men were supposed to want to be.

I had been on the whaling ships many many times, and all without incident. We sailed from the town, and I always knew some of the men from all the other times we had sailed. If it wasn't the fathers, it was the sons, and they just kept coming round as if they couldn't get enough of it. They always said they had to go for the money, but it got into their blood and they could never be rid of it, no matter what they wanted to think.

And I had trouble with it too. I went home when I could no longer put it off, and when the notion of it did not seem so bad. I took my children things that shone, not toys because I could never remember how much they would have grown into men since the last time I saw them, but real things from somewhere beautiful so I could show them how extraordinary the world was.

I took my sister books, because she liked them and because she kept something standing still for me and my brothers who could not stop moving. She had no choice, and we should have let her go too, I sometimes thought. She knew how to tie the winds, and she may have been my undoing, though I cannot believe she would have been so careless, and perhaps it was just my fate to be unlucky that once.

No scholar ever really wrote about Greenland because people who have not been there cannot understand it, and they cannot find the right words to make it live on the page. There are pictures in my sister's books of the mountains of ice that rose out of nowhere if we waited there too long, but they do not show them as they really appear. Now, when I look at them, I can taste only dry breath on my wet tongue, and it takes away the air and leaves a thirst that will not go away.

We weren't far from Greenland on that last occasion when I began to feel uneasy, and I thought something might have happened at home. Home I called it, but it was far from that. I began to wonder, though, what was happening there, and how my sister was, and what ages my children were. Just idle musing which I should not have disturbed as it was better left alone. I was approached by a man who knew me from other times, and he said he knew that look in a man's eye, and that I should ask the Finn.

I did not want to go that far. If I asked the Finn I might find out more than I needed to know, and everyone knew it was dangerous. There are moments in a man's life when he makes a bad choice, and I cannot say whether this was my moment for I do not know whether the result was bad or good, but here I am now to tell the tale.

The Finn was lying awake on his bunk and I had second thoughts, because it was a whim after all. I had been away before and nothing had been amiss at home. There would be word soon enough. But the Finn turned over and faced me, and looked at me with eyes of glass until I asked if he would come up on deck.

He held out his hand, and I placed a coin in it. The hand remained there and I took out two more coins and laid them in his palm. It was dangerous and he needed to make it worth while. I'd heard a story once in a tavern in Hamburg by the harbour, about a man who took away all the rats in a town nearby by piping a tune that led them away. But when he did not receive the payment he had been promised by the town council he piped away their children too, and I did not want the Finn to think I did not value his work.

Finally, he got down from his bunk without looking at the coins, and followed me to a quiet part of the deck. The sun was going down and we had a calm spell, so the men would go below decks until they were needed, maybe until the morning. The Finn asked me questions about my sister's house, about where everything was and what I wanted to know. I remembered the house and its contents not because I had been there often as a man, but because I had grown up there, and assumed little had changed. We had shared everything because there was never two of what we needed.

The Finn took out a piece of chalk and drew a circle on the wooden planks of the deck, then he looked me in the eye, the second time he had done so, and lay down in the circle with his legs flat on the boards. He warned me not to touch him, as it would kill him, and I watched him carefully without knowing what to expect, and wishing I had not asked, as men do when they know they have gone too far. I know now where he went, but at the time I saw only the twitching of his legs and the convulsions which accompanied his deep moan.

He writhed for an hour or more, and I feared someone might come, but no-one did. His fight was with the ether, and he thrashed at the air with his open palms until he collapsed in a heap and was exhausted. He opened his eyes and looked at me from below, then stood up slowly and stepped out of the circle and back onto the deck. He was weary and unsteady on his feet, as if he were drunk, though I knew he had taken no liquor, and he put his hand slowly into his pocket.

I looked him in the eye, expectantly, because even though I knew I had gone too far, I still wanted to know the end of it, like a child with a story when everyone else has gone to bed. He took something out of his pocket and handed it to me, saying, "Your sister is well, but you should not go home."

Telling a man like me he should not go home should have given relief, and made me happy to know I did not need to, but that is not the nature of things. When I was told I should not go home, I was curious, with the same curiosity that made me stay away when I did not need to. I was caught between relief and obligation, because now I knew I could not, it would dog me until I did. I was going to ask him why, and needed an answer so that I could sleep, but the Finn turned around and walked away along the deck, back to the place where I had found him. As he was leaving, he said in his lisping voice, "Call me when you need the boat."

I looked down at the thing he had given me, and saw it was a wooden spoon with a carved top. I had made one like it for my sister years ago, and it always sat in her kitchen by the pot on the fire. I had carved on it the shape of a bird, like the ones that came to nest on the lake in spring and flew away again as soon as they could.

I was in the habit, when I finally lay my head down at night, of dreaming myself to sleep, looking for answers to my questions. That's how I knew what I would do after I had spoken with the Finn. I could not go home, as he said, at least not straight away. I would speak to the skipper, and see what he said about it.

We worked the whales, majestic creatures who defied logic and haunted my nights with their songs and their sadness. We hacked them to pieces and processed their parts, and drained away their blood until we were so exhausted we slept on our feet. But we kept at it because it all came at once, and then we fell asleep, awaiting the boredom and the road home.

That was when I asked to speak to the skipper. He was a man awaiting retirement, and had seen enough of the sea and of men to know I was not to be put off. He appreciated my honesty in asking his permission, and in knowing he could not give it, at least not officially. But he would turn a blind eye if I jumped ship. He left me with a warning though, about Greenland and its winters, because it was not a place where men from my country should like to be and because the customs there were of a nature to be treated with caution.

I did not ask him why, or how he knew, but that same night I took myself away. If I had stolen a boat, I would have been a thief, but the Finn took me ashore and returned before anyone awoke, because at this time there was daylight at all hours and little rest. I made my way to a hut on-shore, and found a corner to curl up in for a few hours, or until I decided what to do, as I did not know this land nor how to treat it. I hoped for kindness and a chance to survive.

I had been there some time when I was aware of a man sitting at the other end of the hut. He was chewing something, but I could not see his face in the half light. His mouth moved, and that was the only sign he was there and not sleeping. I sat up, as I had little to lose, and asked him in English where I might find food and a place to lodge. I had foregone my pay to jump ship, and had only what was with me when I left my country, but the currency was probably worthless for all I knew.

The man stood up slowly, and turned around. He indicated with an imperceptible sweep of his hand that I should follow him, and I gathered up my blanket and did so. We walked out into an empty track, and through a set of buildings, past ships and boats and things of the harbour, and we eventually came upon a road which led away from these reminders of the world I was leaving.

I followed the man as though he were my fate, and we arrived at length at a small quay where he motioned for me to board a boat. The man, I could now see, was a native of these parts, and whether or not he spoke or understood my language was neither here nor there, because he knew where he was going and I had little option but to trust him and my own judgement. I had invited his help, and he had not refused. Only later did I wonder whether he had known I was coming and had been awaiting my arrival.

I sat with him in the small boat which wrapped itself around us, and we set off for a location across the flat water. I took my paddle and joined in the movement of the thing, trying to keep pace with the man's journey, wherever he was going. At some length, after what seemed like hours when I could no longer imagine my feet on land, we arrived at a small inlet, and came in at a narrow beach with stones. After so long sitting, my limbs were sleepy and I had to struggle to take myself out of the wrappings of the boat, and to stand straight on the land. The man pulled the boat in and I bent to help him, but he had the work in hand and did not need me.

With the boat on shore, he motioned for me to follow him, and I clattered through the round beach stones towards a place where smoke was rising from makeshift dwellings. I later knew this to be the camp they made from time to time, between journeys, for it was between journeys that this man had his home, and he had taken me to this place between places to stay. I thought of some of my own people, who would have been reluctant to take in stray men in case they stayed too long, but this man did not live by the same time as those people, and tomorrow and eternity were one and the same.

That is not to say he carried me along. I was always watched in case I did not pull my weight, but as long as I did, I was allowed to follow. I wondered why he had taken me with him, and why he had trusted me when I could have caused him harm, but I discovered during the summers I spent with him that he was an inquisitive man who wished to learn. I had little to teach him because I knew nothing of use to him, but he still asked, and when I could, I answered.

When I arrived at his shelter that afternoon, he went inside and spoke a while with someone, then emerged with a woman, then another. They smiled at me, and indicated that I should enter the hut and lie down to rest on one of the skins lying there on a platform. I was overcome with weariness after my journey, and did as the women said. This is how I came to live with these people and, for a short while, became one of them, because their fears lay in things other than the shape of a man's face.

For the most part, I was grateful to have escaped from the world I found hard to live in. I made a passable living with the Greenlanders, though I lived for some time behind a curtain of ignorance of their ways. Some things do not change in a man for all he would wish them to. I do not know how long I lived and worked with them because after a while I stopped counting the summers and the long winters.

During the summer we left to follow the caribou, and in winter we hunted when we could. I was a curiosity among them, of course, because I did not know their ways, and because I fumbled and worked uncomfortably with their weapons and their tools. The children giggled at my ineptitude and the women smiled, but my friend the man took me very seriously and reprimanded my mistakes so that I would not repeat them when it was dangerous.

He assigned his eldest son to show me how to fish through the ice, and slowly I learned their trades. Only at night came the inquiries about the whalers and where they came from, and why they hunted. I could give them few answers, because I had never thought about it. I had always seen the ships as my work, as an escape from pettiness and the idleness of gossip and judgements. I had given little thought to who gained or lost by them. Sometimes when we were moving, I saw the whaling ships out over the Strait, and I turned away and got on with the task in hand.

I learned to speak the language of these people because I loved the words and their sounds. The words floated through my dreams at night until I devised their meaning, and they remained there for me to use when I wished. It was not just for practical reasons I loved to say their words. It felt like being able to play the fiddle like my brothers, or knowing how to dance with a grace that was mine and mine alone, and slowly I began to speak to these people in a way I had never been able to speak to my own.

One winter, when we were holed up in camp, the man asked me whether I ever wished to return to my family. I turned away for an instant and he knew the answer, so told me that I could not always escape myself, but that my responsibility lay in making choices and, at certain times, I would know what they were. I told him a man had once warned me I should not return home for it was dangerous, but therein lay the dilemma and it had brought on a sickness which would not go away. What a man may not do he stores in his soul until sometimes, when he is old, it makes him fade away. My friend knew this, and said it was time I asked him for help in making a decision.

I had seen what this entailed many times before, and was reluctant to run the gauntlet of a battle with his spirits. I had seen men and women maimed by it and left in half-way worlds from which they could not return. He told me not to be afraid, because I had a strong heart, and he would bring me out of my sleeping and my indecision.

With that, he went to talk to some of the men, and summoned a gathering for he was *angakoq*, a holy man. I was anxious, because I knew like him that there was no escaping the ordeal, and that I would be shaken out of my comfort against my will. I also knew that the alternative was not possible, any more than when I went there in the first place.

A boy was sent to fetch me when the time came, and I followed him to the place where the man, the *angakoq*, sat ready. His hands were bound with rope, as was the custom, and when I had sat down amongst the people, the crowd began to sing low notes. The magus – for this is what my friend had now become – began to speak to his spirits, and came into a frenzy, and I knew then where the Finn had gone to find what he gave me. I hoped never to go there, but that was the fear of men, and I was still, then, a man.

The man writhed and descended up and down in his prison until he had shaken himself free of his chains. Then, briefly, there was a silence and a stillness, and the people around me disappeared and were replaced by a coloured light, dancing around my eyes and into the far distance. The music became slow and floated across my ears and back into the ether as though it were made of it, and wove the colours around my eyes.

I was not afraid, as he had told me I would not be, but felt myself falling into the coloured ether as I would fall into warm water, and I was alone in it but did not care. At length, I think, for there was no day or night in this world, I returned amongst the crowd, and watched as my fate came out to meet me.

The *angaqoq* tapped and inclined until he began to unwind and uncoil into the dance. A bow slithered across a whining gut, slow at first, and then quickening, and faster, and back into the night like a concertina. Smoky images filed past, and out through a hole in the roof, and back down again. Then the magus stepped out in cold shimmer, and many men sang from within him in a low moan. At last, with a triumphant sound of all the cries in the world, he raised his hand and split the notes.

My journey began again at that moment, though I waited a while with these people who had taken me in. I was reluctant to leave them, for I had become comfortable with their comings and goings, and their spirits which would not stand still. But the winter passed, and I knew I could put off my departure no longer.

Within a few months, in the height of summer when the whaling vessels came, I took my leave of the women, then the men, and then the children. Last of all I said goodbye to my friend, the man who had found me, and he smiled and said we would see each other again when I no longer had boats to catch. He took me by kayak to the port where I had spent the night in a hut, however many years ago it had been, and then turned his vessel around and returned whence he had come.

There were many more buildings than I remembered in the harbour, and hives of men milling in and out of them. I struggled to remind myself of my language, though it was not far away in the recesses of my mind, and I asked one of the men if they knew of a Scottish ship that might be in. He replied in Danish, which was not unlike my tongue, and pointed out into the farther reaches of the harbour.

I eventually found what I was looking for, a boat out of Leith, and asked to speak to the skipper. I told him I had been left in Greenland by mistake many years ago, and wished now to return to my country. He would not at first believe me, and asked for papers and more information about where I had been. I told him I had been left onshore when the weather had turned suddenly and winter had arrived early. My crew could not alert me in time and were forced to turn for home, so I was left and had to seek help from the people here. Perhaps I should have told the truth, for either way he would not have believed me.

In the end, though, it turned out he was from my part of the country, and knew some of the people I could name in the town, so he allowed me to travel with him on condition I was responsible for my fate when we touched land. The journey back was smoother than I had hoped, and the men were in good spirits after a profitable season. We arrived at Leith and I evaded the offices on the quay and slipped into the town. I had a small wage the skipper had given me in return for work on the homeward journey, but it would not get me home. It was too little.

In the town though, I had the good fortune to run into people from my part of the country, and they were prepared to advance me the sum required to buy a passage to the north. I could not find a place on the first vessel, but sent word with one of the crew to alert my family to expect me, and finally I managed to secure a place on a small ship with only a few crew, bound for the island.

The journey began badly, with inclement weather and broken machinery, and we had to call in at a port on the way. When we finally hit open sea, our journey became ill-advised, and the weather turned once again, though not gradually, but suddenly, in bursts. We continued, having little recourse but to try and ride out the storm and make land, and the weather showed no signs of abating.

We were not far away from the island when dark sounds began to rumble below deck, and I recognised the look of fear in the men's faces. In a single moment, the waves began to explode under the vessel, and we were so close to shore that the rocks were becoming a danger as we were blown off-course.

The dusk turned into darkness, and we had no recourse to help except on shore. I knew my home by sight, and through the wind I could make out the silhouettes of buildings on the shoreline, but my vision was too distorted to see much more. We must have battled with the storm until we fell asleep with exhaustion, for I found myself waking up in the cold water, clinging to the remains of a broken part of the ship, and daylight was threatening to break through the dark clouds. I could see nothing, and began to drift off, resigned to my fate and briefly recalling the Finn's words. Then, out of the corner of my eye, I saw something solid.

The waves bounced in and out of my vision, but I could see a rock not far away and tried to move towards it. It was too steep to climb onto, but I clung to whatever rough parts I could find that would hold my grip, and I pushed myself round to a spot where I could haul myself up. I could not see far across the land, but had an idea where I had come ashore, so set off in the direction of the nearest dwelling and found it within a mile. I knocked on the door but no-one answered, so I found my way into the byre next to the house. I lay down in some old straw, and there I slept a wandering sleep for a time.

When I awoke, I ventured back to the house, hoping the people had returned from their work or wherever they had been, but still there was no answer. I pushed open the door, but with trepidation, for I had no energy for explanations, and I walked inside the narrow hallway and into the room on the right. I found no life there, but a table laid with cups and a teapot, as though someone had anticipated my coming. I tried the other room, and found two short beds laid with blankets but not slept in.

This was not my house, but the house of a neighbour as I recalled, so I shut the doors behind me in an attempt to hide my presence, and set off down the road to the house which my wife and children kept while I was away. It was mid afternoon, and I would have expected to see people at work but had passed no-one, and the house was quiet and undisturbed.

I pushed open the front door, this time with more force, as this was somewhere I was known. The door did not open at first, and its hinges squeaked and seemed rusty so that I thought it had been neglected in my absence, and I was disappointed in myself for a moment. I opened the door with a stronger push, and finally found myself in the narrow hallway all the houses in this place had. Three coats were hanging on hooks, and I heard the sound of boys' voices coming from one of the two rooms.

Momentarily, I was excited to be home, knowing that it would last only as long as the welcome. I prepared my entrance, sure that by now they must have received the message of my return, and eventually I pushed open the door, anticipating their surprise. But there was no-one in the room. Thinking I had misheard, I tried the door of the other room, which was also empty, yet I continued to hear the voices – voices of boys and men at work, at some task they had to do.

I walked out into the yard and through the byre, and out into the field, but could find no-one. When I returned to the house it was silent, and nothing moved. I walked down the hill to my sister's house, for she, I knew, rarely went any-where, and would be at home. As I walked through the byre door (for I knew it was there I was more likely to find her, and not in the house if she could help it), my foot alighted on something soft and hard at the same time. In the half light between the dark byre and the day, my fingers touched a piece of rope. I picked it up, and found it to be frayed at the edges, and with signs of having been tied and untied many times.

Someone, it seemed, had untied the storm, and we had been wrecked, but I did not believe my sister could have done such a thing. It was an act of irresponsibility and she had no malice, just resignation. I also knew that she was the only one who knew how to tie the winds into submission, and no-one else could have done it. My hurt was tempered by disbelief.

I turned to look across the beach to the sea and, out of the corner of my eye, caught a glimpse of a woman, her skirts passing by with a sound like the wind. When I turned again to look, she had gone, and I was once again alone. I wondered about it for a while, and then I knew I had gone there at last, to the place where the Finn went, but from which he knew how to return. I walked back to where my children's house was, and settled myself into it, though there was no-one there.

I found myself plenty to do and, when there was nothing, I did not even mind the nothing. Occasionally, I went down to the house where my sister lived and took out one of her books, the ones with the pictures, which I had never looked at before, and I read the pictures as though they were a journey back to the places I had been. Sometimes, I saw someone out of the corner of my eye, but they were always gone when I turned, and after a while I gave up trying.

I am still here, and expect to be here for an eternity. It is not a bad place and I miss no-one. Men knowing my story will be sad for my loneliness, which I do not mind. I am not given to sadness. And sometimes when the fire is particularly bright, I see my son, the youngest one, whose name I can never quite remember. He is always at my sister's house, gazing into the books. Once, I swear he caught a glimpse of me too but did not tell a soul.

I put the spoon back in its place by the fire. My sister found it where she had not been able to find it before, and smiled, and I knew she had not wished me ill or untied the knots, and that some terrible accident of bad judgement had occurred. When I would like to see her smile, I take it away again and replace it, so that she knows I am here, and on occasion, she turns and looks around the room for my voice. Long ago, in this place, the dead walked between the walls and the winds, and sat sometimes with the living to talk. Now even the dead are gone, and only I am left to whisper the answers across the divide. ∎

My Aunt - Tying the Wind

There were times in the grey evening, when the sea was reduced to a whisper and the women had gone to bed, that this island became bearable, even good. When our small lives were suspended until morning and we could find a hole to climb in and be ourselves, the place behind the daily grind came into its own and stopped chiding us for our mistakes and our omissions.

At those times, I sat and read the books the men brought me from places I would never see. In summer, I sat on the doorstep and kept company with the waves which were lying in wait in case someone should fail to respect them. They were an uneasy companion, and rose at will. In winter, I sat by the fire or in the corner of the byre if the men were home and filling the house, and there I could find a door into the other worlds if they would let me in.

In the books, I found storms of a different kind, poetry which churned my blood and images which pierced my soul. I travelled on camels and danced on ice, and in the eyes of men caught in the images, I saw a waywardness and a distraction known only to the blind. I heard strange songs caught between the words of the books, sung from the very depth of men's throats, calling their spirits to arms. I sat in cool water on a hot day, and felt it trickle down my back like a man's hand, and all the while, I stepped only through the walls of my confinement, and never once left that place.

I am neither good nor wise. On the contrary, I am on fire and learned to keep a damp flame so as not to offend. I did not begrudge the women their daily lives, but they would have begrudged me mine if they had known the extent of my wanderings. Instead, they held me at arm's length, because that is where they kept people they did not understand and who did not fit into the tidiness they had created for safety. I was careful not to give them clues about the roads I took out of there, because they might have tried to build gates around them. It is extraordinary how adept people are at doing that until they close off even the roads inside a person.

My brothers came and went, and I was their home and their dry land when they could see none. They could move only because I stood still, and I finally became accustomed to their wandering for it was, after all, no different to my own. They had become compulsive and were afraid of being still. I often told them that they must keep walking, because they had not learned to stop without killing their soul, whereas I had the art, and it was my only recourse. They had gone too far to stop.

My nephew, on the other hand, was young, and was beginning to learn. He had taken to the books and preferred them, I think, to the other children's games. It was not a bad thing if this was his inclination, because people should be allowed to incline whichever way the wind blows them. Again though, he no doubt suffered from the boys, and he still has many more mistakes to make. I imagine he will walk after his father, at least for a while. I have only been able to open the spaces to him, and hope that he will find his way from there. I no longer live in permanent dread of what happened, because it is over and has found its level.

The boy's father was my brother, the closest to me in age and in mind. We grew up together on the beach outside the house, and were the ones who found things which others had cast away. They tell me people who do not live close to the sea hear the sound of the waves in sea shells, but we already had the sea, and heard music in the shells when we put them to our ears.

When it was calm, and no-one was looking, we found caves and holes in rocks which led nowhere, and which tapered away into oblivion. Sometimes we walked too far and had to run home after dark, feeling our way through the tall grass on the far side of the beach and hoping for home. And when the sea raged, we danced close to it, inviting it to touch us and not knowing the consequences.

We were the youngest, and allowed to stray, as the youngest often are. It is easier for mothers to get back their breath that way, and easier for fathers to grow old. My father was a quiet man whose status with the crowd was permanently on hold while they waited for him to show signs of doing what men do. The other men did not exclude him, but equally they did not know what to do with a man who did not join them in spirit, and who made no mistakes to be hidden away and denied in unison.

My mother was a woman of little patience, who did not understand my father's silence. She belonged successfully with the other women, in so far as it was possible to do so. All the women live on the edge of self-doubt and constantly suspect others disapprove of them, though they can rarely say why. My mother sank herself into routines because they provided her with the greatest protection from herself.

And my brothers were soon men, and wished to be, though they drifted into manhood without knowing. They were wayward in a different way to me because they needed the sea and it needed them. Only my youngest brother shared my thoughts, played my games and clung to my shadow until he too, in the end, had to go away.

He and I wandered the beach and the edge of the water while the others grew up, and we saw into the rock pools when the sea pulled away. In the rock pools were shadows, and in the shadows were stones, and when the sea pushed its way back in, it all changed shape for ever. The sand shifted and the stones moved, and when we came back to look, it had all gone to another place. That is how I learned to read the tides and to know where the sea went when it left us until the next time.

And when the Minister took it upon himself that the children should learn to read, and took us away from our games and our work, I did not mind. At first, my youngest brother and I went to the school day-about, because it was a long walk and we needed shoes for the stony road, but had only one pair between us. My brother, unlike the older ones, could see the shapes of the letters and retained them in his mind, but his fingers could not write them. In the end he gave up trying, and handed me the torn black boots one day and said, "You go. It's better if you learn it."

And so that's how I learned to read the books they all brought me, and know about the world. I knew when boats left Bari for Greece, and how to set the table in a grand house. I knew what names to address a king by and what the wind is called in Africa. I knew that, in America, there were forests as thick as a horse's mane, and trees the size of houses. I learned about strange ships in China and paper houses in Japan, and I saw how men walked on stilts to dance.

When I had read the books, I read them again, and sometimes again, and then I knew that in Australia there were people like me, black men who saw shifting colours in the desert, just as I saw them in the wind and in the sea, and who knew how to live by them. In Siberia, where the winds rose at will and carried off men's souls as they can here, I learned that there were men and women whose hard duty it was to level spirits and stop them from taking men away forever, and I knew I was not alone.

Until I read those books, I had been afraid of what happened one day on the beach with my brother. That was the day I slipped into the world I would never be rid of. At times, I wished I could give it up or give it back, but that is not how it works. It is there with me now for ever, and I have learned to live with it.

We met a man sitting on a rock, with a sack tied around his shoulders and under one arm, who was carving something, a piece of blue stone, and who looked up as we approached. We stared at him a while, as children are apt to do who have no grace, and he raised his eyebrows and then looked down and continued his work. At length, my brother spoke and asked him what he was making, and the man looked up again. He said it was a gift, and that we were to tell no-one.

He asked if we would like to sit with him a while until he finished his work, and he would tell us a tale from somewhere we could not have been. He seemed to be a tall man, though he was sitting, and had long black hair tied behind his head with a dark ribbon. He had a quiet face, and was neither young nor old, neither bright nor dim, but he was slightly crooked as he sat and we felt sorry for him, so stayed a while. We thought he must have come from a ship, here for a while and then gone again. He was ragged though, and had an exotic air that made us stay, for we were both wayward, even then.

He did not smile much at all. On the contrary, he was evasive and we were afraid of him at first. He told us he had come to fetch something, and would not stay long, but that we could sit and talk to him if we liked. He began to talk of places where no men go, magical places caught between the ether, where shadows of people come and leave as if they are travellers who cannot stop. He spoke of feet that could not help walking and fiddles that could not help playing, and as he spoke my brother's eyes grew wider and more fixed on the man.

I tugged at my brother's sleeve and tried to drag him home, but he would not come. The man saw my distress and said we had nothing to fear, and that if we stayed a while he would show me a trick. He would teach me how to hold down the waves. I hesitated long enough for him to pull out from his pocket a piece of rope, and tie first one knot in it, and then another, and then a third. Then he looked me in the eye, and I saw in his face an eternity and a flicker of something beyond the horizon, but also an earnestness, and knew he would tell me no more unless I listened and took heed.

I was a careful child, growing already into adolescence, and I knew that this was no trick. The man was giving me something important, so I stood up straight and waited for him to tell me what to do. He took the rope and dangled it in front of my eyes, and said that if I untied the first knot it would release a breeze and speed the boats along a little faster. I must think carefully before untying the second knot because it would give a boat good speed, but it would let loose a wind only the good sailors could ride and it may not take them home.

He fell silent, and though I was not given to asking adults questions because they hardly ever gave me a straight answer, I asked him what the third knot was for. His face darkened and a shadow passed over it, and at first he looked away. He stared into the air across the sea and finally turned to me and said that on no account was I to consider untying the third. It was there as a buffer between me and myself, and if I chose to tie the knots I must live with the consequences.

My brother was enchanted, but a shiver ran down my spine and I thanked the man and turned round to go home. My brother, though, did not follow, and I took him by the arm and forced him away. His legs came, and ran alongside mine, but his eyes stayed behind with the man, and when we reached home he said nothing, and my mother could not rouse him. She put him to bed thinking he had caught a chill, and wrapped him in a blanket.

The next morning when I awoke and scrambled to the fire to catch the embers before they died, my brother was awake, and carrying in water from the well. He seemed in good humour, with no trace of fever, but still had a faint far look in his eye. He told me he had been to visit the man, who had shown him the house in the hill where he lived, and I dropped the poker into the fire.

My brother told me the man, when he stood up, was not tall, but stunted. He had been kind, and had given him soup to drink, soup such as he had never tasted before, and the man's house had been warm. It had seemed small from the outside, cut out of the rock into the hillside, but as they entered, it revealed itself to be a larger space, with rooms off into the hill. My brother had never seen such a place before, only the stone houses we lived in, and he asked the man why he had never seen him there. The man had told him he rarely ventured out, as he had his work indoors and could not stay out for long.

When my brother had realised he should go, as it may be getting late and even he did not cross certain thin lines, he took his leave and thanked the man. As he reached our house on the edge of the beach, he picked up the empty bucket lying at the gate and filled it in the well before coming in.

He believed himself to have arrived home that very moment, as I got up to light the fire from the embers, and he had, he thought, been gone but a short while.

I knew better than to call my mother as she had no time for our distractions, and I told my brother to take the bucket and put it in the corner until we needed it. Then I asked him to take me and show me where the man lived, because I wanted to ask him again how to tie the knots in the rope. My brother was unaware of the dawn which should have been night, and he took me by the hand to the beach. At the end of the long sand, where it gave way to rocks and curved around into the sea, he turned up onto a path that led away into the hill where we only went at peat-digging time.

The path was wet and slippery with the dew, and got steeper as we went further from the beach because places like this are not for the faint-hearted. My feet slipped on the sharp stones along the path and I had to crawl in places, using my hands to maintain a grip. As we neared a ledge, I was aware of a hand reaching down to take mine, and it was a large hand and strong, not my brother's.

I did not dare look up for fear of falling, but did not take the hand at first because it would have been too easy to do so, and I was suspended between the sky and the sea. When I could no longer go neither forwards nor backwards, I gripped the long fingers and allowed myself to be pulled up.

The man was there as he had been on the beach the day before, but was tall and elongated, or so it seemed to me, quite unlike what my brother had said. He pulled me towards him and onto the ledge, and it was only then that I realised my brother had not followed me along the full length of the path. The man's eyes told me I was to walk with him. He inclined his head gracefully, and slightly, and he smiled.

I should have been afraid, as I was not a naïve child and was nearing the age where I knew about men and what they asked. I had seen my brothers dancing with the women when the sea gave them leave, and I watched the look in their eyes and the twitching of their hands and their loss of reason. I knew this man was a stranger now, but would not be forever, and his invitation was not of the kind my brothers gave to their women.

He led me through a small door into the hill, which opened upwards as though it were the covering of a crooked well, and I entered a dark room down a ladder. My eyes tried to adjust to the low light, but the darkness was warm and safe. The room was filled with rocks of different shapes and sizes, some white like the outcrops on the other side of the island, and some blue or green and rounded by their years of playing with the sea.

Some of the blue and green rocks were carved into the shape of seals and whales, and some looked like boats and men. Some were small, and some were whole chunks cut out of the hillside, and were almost alive. The white rock stood up in sharp mountains of crystal and towered up from the floor to flicker with the candlelight on the walls. Hanging from the ceiling were pieces of rope winding in and out of chunks of the white rock, the whole suspended between the place I had left and the place I was now.

For the first time, I looked at the man's face, and it was dark and shadows passed over it, but there was a light in his eyes such as I had never seen in a person before. His hair was long and black, and it was tied behind his head with a dark ribbon like the tinkers used to do, and for a while that was what I thought he was. But I did not hide from his gaze as I did from theirs, and he wished me no harm.

He asked me if I knew where the day went when it became night, and if I knew where the snow went when it melted. He asked me a lot of questions but did not give me the answers, nor did I ask for them. I could not turn and leave this man, and my eyes began to follow his across the pages of the stories he read me from memory.

All the while he was talking to me, the silence around him grew deeper, and the other objects in the room, though there were few, faded out of my vision. At length he stood up and asked me to come nearer the fire, and he took my hand once again. He placed in it a piece of rope, with three knots, and then took my head in his hands and kissed me slowly on the forehead with a warmth I shall never know again. He told me never to return unless I needed him, because he was never far away, but I would not find him by looking.

At this, he helped me climb the wooden ladder out of the house, and followed me until I reached the ledge. He helped me down the narrow path, which this time was easy, and I did not fall as I had on the way up. As I neared the beach, I turned around and saw that the man was gone.

From the moment I sat for a while with this man, I have loved him and him alone, and cannot look at other men who are pale and without substance. The island men disgust me with their fear and their fumbling. They are like a damp oven which will not light, and walk carefully through their lives like the sheep they tend. They are afraid to want, in case they might fall over the edge, and then they become sick, until they are sad and old, and die before their time.

That night I slept soundly, in a warm place where there was no wind, and the sky was a deep blue. I walked through endless dreams and could not be roused when morning came. My mother was concerned and tried to get me to sit by the fire, which I eventually did, but with little strength. When my mother saw I was not unwell,

she smiled, and knew I had become a woman.
Like all mothers, she had forgotten it would be so
soon.

In the afternoon, though, when the quiet came,
and we had time to think before we went on with
life, I went back across the beach, in trepidation,
for this time it was my choice. I followed the path
I had taken the day before, but it was neither
steep nor difficult, and I realised I had not come
the right way. I tried many, many times after that
to find the path, but could not, and it became a
secret, even to myself. I knew it would dissolve
with the telling, and no-one has ever heard it until now.

With the passing of time, I stopped trying to
find the path, but never forgot that it was there
somewhere. Only many years later did I find it
again, because I needed to speak with the man,
and I knew he was the only one who could help
me. When my brother disappeared and I found
the rope lying untied beneath the bed, I knew
what had happened, and that, only that once, I
had been unguarded long enough to cause harm.
My nephew did not know what he was doing, because I had only ever told him half the story, and

he found the knots where he should not have been looking.

When I knew what had happened, after the storm, I wondered at first whether I was wrong. At times my brother would come back, and appear in the room by the fire, but I could not keep him there, and only saw him out of the corner of my eye. When I turned to look, he had gone. He was living alone between the walls of our houses, and did not know how to leave nor how to return, and I realised, as time went on, that I had no recourse but to go to the man I had known that day on the hill.

This time I knew I would not have to look for him, and that he would be there as he had promised. I climbed the steep rock, this time a woman and no longer a child. His hand came out again to meet me, and lifted me onto the ledge where his house began, and we sat a while outside in silence, my legs dangling over the side of the ledge down towards the sea. At length, I turned to look at him, and he smiled as he had done when I first met him, and I returned his smile with a warmth I had nearly forgotten how to light.

He said he had been waiting for me, and knew I would come to find my brother. He did not need to ask me if I knew the consequences, or whether I feared them, for he knew I came willingly, and that I was glad for the chance to do so after trying for so many years to forget. I was in no hurry, and neither was he, for we had an eternity. At length, he took my hand and led me past the house and beyond the ridge, towards a high promontory beyond where we cut and stacked the peat.

From there, I watched a man walking slowly away from us, along the beach and towards my house. As he approached, my nephew stood on the steps watching his father's progress. By the time the man reached the rocks, my nephew was walking out to meet him, because he knew this man a little, though he could not remember how. At length, the two returned to the house, and may have stayed there a while together, maybe for some time, I do not know, for my brother was now a free man, whether he wished it or not. He had reasons to return to the world where I had none to stay.

I turned to the man standing beside me in the high place, and this time I offered him my hand.

He took it and pulled me towards him, until we felt the wind a little on our backs and sought the warmth of his house. I had, when all was said and done, finally come home. ■

The Ornithologist

It took six and a half years to find Billy Johnson and bury him, and even then it did not occur to anyone that something had been lost. After a while they had given up looking for him and assumed the sea had taken him far out, and eaten his flesh and eroded his bones and what was left of him down to nothing at all. And by that time, there was really no-one who needed to find him.

Eventually, one day, a tangled body turned up on the beach, the one where no-one ever went because it was hard to get to by land, and someone noticed it from a boat. It had been lying there on the wet sand as if the life had only just left it, and no-one knew how this could be because Billy had disappeared a long time ago, and his body along with him. Nothing like this had ever happened before.

The men were called and the authorities were contacted, and the body was taken away. Never had so many people been interested in the fate of Billy Johnson and never would they be again, and for a short while he became the centre of attention. Doctors examined his body expecting to determine when and how he died, but no-one could, and this was a problem because the courts and the newspapers and all the people who moved files from one cabinet to another needed answers so that they could close the case and move on.

But Billy would not lie still, though he himself would have had no wish to detain them. He had no use for them at all where he lived and died. The doctors were puzzled because Billy's body had stopped living a very long time ago. Not a few days ago, as the fishermen had thought when they found it, and not six years ago when he disappeared, but many years ago, more than made any sense to anyone. Until the enigma was solved, no-one could bury him and he was costing the authorities money.

Investigations brought them no further to the truth, despite weeks of long hours and frayed tempers, and at length Billy's body was released for the funeral so that it could lie alongside his mother's and father's and his grandmother's. If it had been left to the people Billy knew, there would not have been a large crowd, but the tiny stone church, perched on the rock in the shifting sands, could not hold the crowds of journalists and greedy eyes which descended on it, and some had to stand outside.

The Minister tried his best to find information about Billy's life so that he could deliver the appropriate tribute, but he had not been able to find anyone who knew him well enough to say anything, so he waxed instead about the only thing anyone knew about him.

"Billy Johnson loved birds. He wandered the hills to photograph them with the camera his father bought him, and since he did not have much education..." here the Minister was quick to add that no-one did when Billy was a child, just in case it came out wrongly, "... the camera was his constant companion." Then he announced a hymn, as he could not think of much else to say, Billy not having been a particularly regular member of the congregation.

At length, Billy Johnson's body was lowered into the ground, and the digital photographic equipment flashed for a few seconds, and then, to all intents and purposes, he was gone. Everyone repaired to the village hall for a reception laid on by a local committee, because the place had not received so much attention since the oil spill. It was going to be a good night.

After they all left, the walled cemetery once again became the resting place of tired minds whose time had come and gone. It whispered a little to the sounds of the sea and the wind, but mostly it remained still and acquiesced because it was easier that way. While the bodies rotted, the souls sometimes came out to dance, because dancing was allowed when the daily world was not looking or would not see.

On the other hand, Billy's story brought people to the village who had not known it was there, and sometimes people bought houses there because it was not as far from the city as they had thought, and they could go there at weekends, or when their children had school holidays, and so the village did not fade away as everyone had thought it would.

In fact, people whose fathers and mothers had moved away to the city to give themselves better chances in life, and to find work when there was none in the village, started to come back, to find what they thought their parents had left behind. Eventually, their parents came back too, tired and with less urgency, and they lived out their last days where they had been born.

On the other hand, this created a problem for the authorities because when these people died they had to be buried, and very soon there was not enough room in the graveyard. The authorities' wheels cranked and creaked into motion, and after a few years the order finally came through to extend the cemetery outwards, away from the sea and beyond the stone walls of the enclosure. Machinery came in and rumbled its way through the rocks which had stood for a long time without moving, and they were sorry but they would have to remove, with as much dignity as they could, the graves immediately alongside the wall.

The village worthies were not too worried. Those graves were Johnsons and none of them were left alive to mind or to be offended. Besides, this was just the "foreign quarter" where the incoming families lay, those who had moved into the village less than 200 years ago from places indeterminate, somewhere else. This unusual segregation of the graveyard worked well enough for the first generation, separating bloodlines in death as in life, but no-one had thought what would happen when the incomers married villagers. Then the dilemma arose of where the foreign spouses and their children would be buried, with their native partner or parent, or in the appropriate quarter? It was, however, generally decided by an unofficial evaluation of character, and if the body passed the test, it was allowed into the hallowed ground.

When the bulldozers moved in, they were given careful instructions not to stray into the "old" section, otherwise the village dignitaries could not be responsible for the consequences. If Mr. Wilkinson from the City Council had not been there checking on progress while this happened, no-one might have noticed that only four coffins came out of the ground instead of five in the Johnson plot.

One had no writing on it at all, but was very old, and he deduced that belonged to number 2314 on the list. In fact, it was Billy's grand-mother, or rather, what was left of her. The one next to that must have been the grandfather, whom no-one really remembered. The two marked ones were his mother and father, and they were easy enough to confirm, but nowhere could anyone find Billy's. It should have been the most recent, and it was not there, but since this was not an exercise in locating graves but one in transferring them, the men only needed to account for what came out of the ground, not what should have been there. So it was not spoken about.

Years later, however, when Mr. Wilkinson retired, he rented a small cottage in the village, and prepared for quiet years indulging his interest in cataloguing the local flora. He was made welcome by villagers, who remembered his respectable career, and he spent many evenings in neighbours' houses recalling an anecdotal past. It was, after all, a good place for memories.

On one such occasion, when he was visiting an old friend, Billy Johnson's name was mentioned and, as an aside and half in jest, Mr. Wilkinson recalled the time he had been supervising the extension of the graveyard.

"You know," he said, savouring a digestive biscuit, "we couldn't find Billy's coffin when we opened up the Johnson plot. It was curious. Someone must have documented it wrongly, because it had to be there, but we didn't have time to extend the trench and we never found it."

His neighbour, who had been preparing a pot of tea, stopped for a moment, and Mr. Wilkinson wondered whether she had been listening. He was on the verge of changing the subject when the woman turned around and said, "It doesn't really surprise me."

"Who was Billy anyway?" Mr. Wilkinson asked. "Was he born here?"

"Oh yes," began the story. "Billy was born here, but he was a bit strange and nobody ever really knew him very well. In fact, when he disappeared, it was about two weeks before anyone noticed – I think it was the postman who finally raised the alarm because he couldn't get the door open for the pile of unopened mail in Billy's porch. We don't know where he went. You'll remember what big news it was when Billy disappeared, and even when his body turned up no-one could get to the bottom of how it happened. He must have drowned, of course, and maybe that was just Billy, not very cautious, falling over the cliff watching the birds. But we never did find out. It all just died down when no-one came up with any answers."

And so, little by little, Mr. Wilkinson heard about Billy Johnson, and was much the wiser for it. And many years later when he, of all people, found out where Billy had gone, he went to lay flowers on the place where his grave should have been. He thought, in doing so, he might bring him back for a few moments, so that Billy could show him the road home.

* * * * * * *

From the moment he was born, Billy Johnson was never alone. His mother had died the same day he entered the world, and his father's will had left with her, so that all that was left was the part of him that went out to work in the fields in the morning and came home tired at night. Billy was brought up by the wind and the passing ghosts.

The boy, even when he was very small, watched birds. He did not count them or make notes on their habits, nor did he steal their eggs or shoot them for the pot. Billy watched the birds and knew them well, though no-one ever benefited from that but Billy himself. On mornings of light drizzle or latent sunshine he took himself off into the hills and sat on rocks made of quartz and granite, and he watched as the different birds of all shapes and provenance came and went.

When he watched them he had a slight tick along the left side of his face. He did it because he could not quite help it, or no longer wished to, and because it held the birds steadier. With his face convulsing in its strange jerking motions, the birds sat stock still in the sky on the other end of his line of vision.

He had no binoculars, just his naked eye, and he had learned to bring the floating birds closer by lining them up with a focal point somewhere inside himself. He could see even the smallest of them away off in the distance because his vision could walk the straight tightrope to where they were hiding and fly along with them in the grey sky, like a long kite.

Billy Johnson grew up with his father because there was no-one else to take care of him. His father had no idea how to look after a baby, but the occasional neighbour helped, and he managed by setting the child in a cradle near the fire until he came back from doing whatever he had to do, and hoping nothing went awry in the meantime.

These arrangements worked well enough before Billy learned to walk, and then his father had to tie him to the wall on a long rope attached to a large metal ring, so that he would not fall in the fire. One day, though, when the boy was old enough to be frustrated, he got loose, or the rope wasn't tied tightly enough, whichever. When his father came home from bringing in the cattle for the night, Billy was ambling around the room with his thumb in his mouth, and his father was afraid he might have hurt himself on the hearth with the stray flames.

"All right," the boy said. "Granny came."

The fact that his grandmother had been dead nearly a decade was immaterial to both Billy and his father, and this became a normal state of affairs in their daily life. The old woman came and sat with him, and told him stories while she rocked in the chair by the fire, and in exchange, Billy sat still and did not fall into the flames. When he was a little older, he asked her about waders and hawks and birds of the sea. He did not know their names, so she told him. She came and sat with him until he was about seven and she had assured herself he could fend for himself, and then, one day, she got up from the chair and did not return.

In this world of lost dimensions where Billy grew up with ghosts, real was what he made it. He danced through his childhood with oblivion and had nothing in common with other boys. He had a soft spot for Red-throated divers and Oystercatchers, and Herons when they came sometimes. He could not find a gift for drawing the creatures and did not really want to, because he only thought to watch them. His father, though, worried about this and considered the matter carefully. If Billy could find a useful talent, the world might be more willing to treat him kindly.

His father emptied all the money he had saved in the pot in the cupboard and bought a simple camera so that Billy could make photographs of the birds and maybe sell them sometimes in summer. The camera was a cumbersome black box, and came along with thick glass slides and an instruction book which neither of them could understand. The first time he saw the camera, Billy turned it around in his fingers and looked at all its nooks and corners, and then he took it into the light outside the sombre house and gave it a more thorough going over. It was almost too big for his small fingers, and it took him a while to grasp it and turn it over a few times.

At length, he took it back inside and looked at his father. "Is this for the birds?" he asked, and his father nodded. The grown man knew all too well that it would not change things, only that it might give his son some comfort if all else failed. Billy set the camera down on the table and did not pick it up again until the following day, when he began to examine the box of glass slides and apparatus that came with it.

No-one ever knew how he worked out how to use it, how all the pieces fit together and how he turned them into pictures. No-one could ever work out how he could get so close to the birds and take them from such angles, but somehow he managed to create images such as no-one had ever seen before. The birds were looking at themselves in the camera, and seemed to be climbing out of their own image. At times, they became spectres on the raw landscape and floated in and out of line with the horizon. Sometimes, you could almost swear they moved slowly across the photograph and landed on the other side.

Everyone who saw the pictures was transported for a moment into the place where birds live, but because this was not particularly useful, they did not like to go there often, and Billy was considered to be something of a fool. He would never amount to much, and no-one gave him much hope. Those who were of a kindly disposition smiled at his photographs and humoured him, but smiled again when they turned away so that others might think them indulgent but not foolish. Those of a less kindly nature asked him if he was "out with his birds" or "away off with the fairies again" because they knew it would make people laugh.

This was all very well. Billy's face did not change much whichever way they did it, and he went off to talk with his ghosts. There was, however, a minor compensation for the heckling in the village. Because there was nothing much you could do with boys like Billy, people left them alone and did not try to make them too useful. There is a difference between usefulness and respect, but we all too often equate the two.

In the mornings, anyone who rose early to get the work done and gain a reputation for themselves as a hard worker sometimes saw Billy wandering the edges of the coastline or the hills behind the village. He was not hovering or rushing or straining to catch the birds. He was just walking at a level pace, swinging his camera by its strap and occasionally, when the mood took him, standing still and staring upwards for a while. Periodically he took his camera, not because he had seen a bird or because there was anything unusual there at all, but because he had decided it was time. When he lifted the camera upwards, a bird always appeared across its viewfinder, and sat there in suspension long enough for Billy to borrow its image and talk with it a while. Then he walked on to another place, or no place at all.

In their cottage, small and cluttered as it was, Billy's father made him a darkroom in a cupboard below the stairs. No-one knew how the boy worked out the procedures, or indeed whether he followed them the same way others did, but somehow at the end of it all, images appeared on glass slides and paper which almost could not have been there, because they were beautiful and did not seem to have been made by men.

Someone, however, did notice Billy's photographs, and offered him the use of a room in his large house to work on them, and a cupboard to store them in. The man was wealthy, and lived in the village because he owned much of its land. He was also a doctor, one of considerable achievement in his day, who understood the rarity of intelligence because he had seen how most men feel safer within the mediocre.

He met Billy early one morning when their paths coincided and no-one else was awake, and he had a sense that he was in the presence of greatness. He asked deferentially if he might stand with him a while and contemplate the morning. Billy looked into his eyes and nodded, but did not think it odd. Neither spoke, nor felt the need to, but the doctor watched Billy with some interest as he occasionally took one of his photographs. Before they parted company, he asked the boy if he might see the finished images, as he himself had something of an interest in photography.

Billy rarely questioned people's motives because he was ingenuous, and took the images to the doctor's house a few days later. The doctor had been brought up to speak respectfully to all things, whether they be good or bad, mild or ill tempered and whether they be rich or poor, and he welcomed the boy with a slight bow, indicating with his hand that he should come in. Most of the village people considered it a privilege to enter the doctor's house, and they simpered a little because this is how they showed their respect. Billy had none of these affectations and the doctor found this a relief because he was not a pretentious man and wearied at times of maintaining his distance from other men.

Billy showed the man his birds on paper, and the doctor looked patiently through the photographs as Billy explained, in his rather stilted speech, what the name of each bird was, and how his grandmother had told him. Unlike the others, the doctor did not flinch when Billy mentioned his grandmother, because whether or not the boy talked to ghosts was immaterial to him, and not the reason he was there. Nor did the doctor mention Billy's facial peculiarities or suggest a therapy, partly because it was only others who felt the discomfort, and partly because he had seen enough illness to know it was not a deep hurt.

This was when the doctor asked the boy if he would do him the honour of transferring his work to the darkroom in the big house, and allowing him to see the photographs whenever they were ready. It is all the man wanted, to be able to see the images, and any more would have been too much. He did not ask Billy to show them to the world, or to send them to the great institutions of the cities, or to sell them to the visitors. He simply wanted to see them, and to allow himself the luxury of departing into the skies beyond the paper birds for just an instant each time.

So Billy took his glass plates and his papers and his photographs to the doctor's house, and the village people chattered about it as they were wont to do. The arrangement went on for many years, and each time a new image appeared, the doctor stopped whatever he was doing and sat down in comfort to enjoy the journey where it began. Occasionally, he accompanied Billy in the early morning along the cliffs, and sometimes they met by chance, and though neither ever said much, their lives merged in a respectful place where words are not required.

When Billy was fourteen, or so everyone judged, because no-one could remember when he was born – his father died quite suddenly of a stroke. He was out one day with the cattle, something routine, and he did not return. Billy was developing photographs in his darkroom under the stairs and his father came along to tell him he had to leave now. By the time the men came to tell Billy, the boy and his father had already said goodbye for what each knew would be a little while.

His father was buried in the plot alongside Billy's mother, where he had been anyway for some time. Billy did not visit the graves to put flowers on them like the other people in the village did for their parents or their grandparents or sometimes their children. Instead Billy resumed his morning walks along the cliff top with his camera, and people took this to mean he was too simple to grieve. Had it been anyone else, he would have been chastised for not grieving properly.

As the roads into the village improved, and people in the cities became more comfortable, visitors began to appear along the beach in summer, people who wanted to spend their holidays in a quieter place where there were no distractions. Some of them met Billy on his walks, and the braver ones talked to him and asked him about his camera, just as the doctor did.

Some of the visitors returned year after year, and came to have a stake in the place because they knew it a little better than others. They knew the names of its birds and its spring flowers, and they had even made friends there and went to call on them, because they wished to hear stories which people had forgotten how to tell in their daily world. Their constancy, year after year, also made them known to the villagers, who welcomed them back each time as though they were the sun returning after a spell of rain.

Some of these visitors became Billy's friends, and they made a point of visiting his house to hear news of the birds. They brought him dates and sometimes Brazil nuts, which he was fond of and could not afford with his small income from the land. Billy always welcomed them with a smile and a slight nod of his head, though he said little.

He took them to see the birds, or showed them his photographs, and always they walked together or sat together in a silence which did not offend. Even after Billy had long gone, the visitors came, until the village became too crowded and no longer held for them the charm of isolation. When the visitors left each year and the winter came, the quiet times set in, and the young man walked the cliffs in the morning and sat with the doctor and the birds in the small world.

The older man cleared out a whole room of his house, leaving in it only a small desk and a large set of shallow wooden drawers, stacked on top of one another and reaching from one wall to the other. They were intended for catalogued specimens of all kinds of things, and he asked Billy if he wished to keep the glass slides in them, so that he would know where to find each one at a glance.

The boy was captivated by the small wooden drawers. In fact, he had never been so taken with anything before. He subsequently spent hours locked away in the room, sorting out glass slides and slotting them into places where he would find them again. Only Billy knew the logic of the order they were stacked in, and he could always locate exactly what he was looking for at a moment's notice.

Sometimes, the doctor asked if they could bring out a hawk, or a particular photograph he remembered of a diver or a curlew. The boy always went straight to the drawer where it lay, brought out the box containing the slide and one containing its print, and set the two out alongside one another on a round table they kept for showing the birds. The doctor would smile and sit down in the chair at the table, and watch the bird fly across its own shadow until the image came into perfect focus, and then he closed his eyes and dreamed for a little while. Sometimes he brought Billy a cup of tea, and they sat together and peered out of the long glass windows of the veranda until the sun set in their place without words.

At some point along the years, when Billy was of an age where most boys were expected to be useful, the doctor fell ill, and both he and Billy knew that he would not live long. He told Billy he should take away his photographs and keep them carefully, because he was not sure that the nephews and nieces who would move into his house would have the same understanding of them. So Billy took it all back to where it had started out, under the stairs of his cottage, and went each evening to the dying man's house to show him the old images and the new images, and this way, the doctor did not feel the pain.

There came a day when the old man could not open his eyes any more, and Billy sat beside him and held his hand, and was stoical and resigned because he did not see where the line was drawn between where the doctor was and where he was going. The old man whispered to Billy that he could still see the birds, somewhere in the place where he was and the place where they were hiding, and he thanked his friend for showing him how to get there. It was, he said, just the same as ever.

The doctor slid away, along the path Billy had shown him, but often returned to talk with him on his early morning walks. They stood and watched until the sun rose, or the skies darkened with cloud, and eventually the birds always came and sat with them for a while.

After the doctor had been buried for many years and Billy had somehow carried on with a small income from his cows, something happened which no-one had expected. Billy rarely received mail, except from one or two of the visitors who were confirmed letter-writers by habit, but things still arrived for him from the offices of the city where the men and women spent their days addressing bills and demands to strangers. One by one, these missives built up in a pile behind Billy's door, unopened and unanswered, until the postman, who let himself into people's houses as he had always done, could no longer open the door. At first, he thought Billy was just himself, not so bright and not able to keep a tidy house and a tidy mind, and he just kept leaving the letters on the stone floor inside the porch. Eventually, however, he called Billy to the door, and when there was no answer, he went in and wandered through the house to find him, thinking he had better take a look in case something was wrong.

In the house were Billy's teacups on the table, unwashed and a little chipped, but that was not unusual because he did not have the habit of washing them after he had used them. On the floor were the old flagstones, a little muddy and unswept, and in the darkened bedroom his old iron bed was unmade, as though he had just stepped out of it and gone to the cattle shed. The curtains were drawn, and the postman stepped inside the room to open them, in case he had missed something.

The postman had never seen inside this room before, and as he turned around to face it, he saw something no-one had seen. The walls were covered in photographic prints of birds, overlapping and turned inwards on themselves with the damp. They were large and small, either in stark black and white outline with a light which almost shone through them, or curiously, with no image at all. All the images were in black and white, though most people took colour photographs by this time, and the light shining from behind each bird made them stand out on the paper in a way which did not need colour.

The postman, strangely, did not recognise any of the birds in the photographs, as they were not from the area at all, but he had seen some of them in books or magazines. There were auks and humming birds, perhaps a parrot, and something which looked like a crane, but the postman was not knowledgeable in these matters and so did not linger on each image long. He assumed at first that the photographs were clippings from magazines or had been sent to Billy by some of the visitors who came in summer to see him, but something told him they had been taken by Billy himself, as his photographs always seemed to have looked that way.

The postman began to feel cold, and stepped back out into the sunshine. He conferred with the people in the village, who had not seen Billy for some time, and they all agreed they should call the police, as Billy had clearly disappeared and could be in trouble. Their concern was evident, but no-one seemed to know what to do because when a problem is real and not gossip, people become weak.

The policemen came eventually, and searched the house and the land around it for signs of Billy.

They found nothing the postman had not seen, but collected a few pieces of what they considered evidence into small plastic bags, and someone marked them with a number. When one of the men opened a wooden wardrobe, however, he discovered a mountain of small, neatly stacked cardboard boxes, which he opened and took to the window for light. They were heavy, and weighed down his hand, so that he wondered what could be inside and, for the sake of procedure, called over a colleague just in case. He prised the thick paper lid from one of them, and found inside a number of large, black, glass plates. He did not know what they were, because he was not a photographer and did not know that, many years ago, this is how photographs were made.

The policemen returned to the wardrobe and discovered that it was full to the brim of hundreds of the same boxes, all of which contained the glass plates. They packed a few of them into crates and had them taken to the city where someone could examine them in more detail, and it may or may not tell them something they wished to know, Then they set off to call the Coastguard, because they feared the worst.

The Coastguard helicopter combed the sands and the seas for a few days, and found nothing, nor was there any response to calls for people who had seen Billy, despite newspaper coverage and even some interest from the regional television station. When his neighbours were asked about his character, all they could say was that he never caused any trouble, and was a quiet, reserved man who had lived in the village all his life. No-one mentioned what they were thinking, that he was not the same as them, and that he was always wandering, though some did venture a theory that he was given to morning walks and may have slipped over the cliff.

As the weeks passed, searches were called off and the media turned their attention to the economy and strikes and the closure of factories and people's livelihoods. In the City Council, a man was found guilty of accepting favours, and it seemed as if the spell of wet weather would never end.

In a small, family photographic shop in the city's old quarter, which had been running since time immemorial but whose customers now were limited to those with a serious interest, a man had been commissioned by the police to develop a selection of the glass plates, just so they could allay whispers. The old man was engrossed in the slides and took long hours to work on them after closing time, because it had been a long time since he had been allowed to indulge in such a pleasure.

Slowly, the images appeared from the slides, and revealed birds of species which made little sense and which could not have been, so the old man rushed them first to a friend who still knew about these things. His friend spread the images out on a table and took a good look at them.

"Are you sure these came straight from the glass slides?" he asked. "Could they have been taken from a drawing or something?"

"I doubt it," replied the old man who knew his craft. "They seem to have been taken from life – you can feel the life in them. They don't even look like drawings."

"I would tend to agree with you." came the response. "But of course it doesn't add up. All these birds died out long ago and could never have been around during the lifetime of the photographer, even if he had been to the places where they were found. "Look at this one, for example. It's a Great Auk. I'll check, but I'm fairly sure. No-one's seen them since the 1840s or '50s, and I don't think there are any photos of them. Look at its eyes. They're quite real. It's the thing that bothered Darwin you know, the eyes. He couldn't quite get to the bottom of them."

"I must admit, it had occurred to me there was something odd about the images," said the old man, not a little perturbed. What do you suppose we ought to tell the police? There's not much we can tell them that would make much sense."

"I would just hand them the prints. I suppose they only want to see that there's nothing illegal on them, and I can't imagine they'd be interested in much else. It would only complicate matters for them. I'd like to know if you find anything out about them though – interesting how it's been done."

It did not for one moment occur to the expert that anything but trickery could be involved, because he had built his knowledge of birds on a solid foundation. He gave it some thought now and then after that, but not enough to see through to the answers. The slides and the prints went back to the police, and the men heard no more about them. Occasionally, though, when the old man from the photography shop was tired, and it had been a long day with people asking tedious questions, he fancied he saw the dark shape of an auk ambling across his vision behind the old wooden cupboards of his shop, and he closed his eyes and smiled.

The police put the slides back in the wardrobe where they had found them because someone, sooner or later, would inherit or buy the house they supposed, and besides, this was the procedure. There was, however, no such tidy end to the mystery of Billy's body until men in a fishing boat discovered it on the beach, six and a half years later. The body was taken in and examined and turned over many, many times, and teams of experts argued over it and disputed one another's theories. Still no-one knew what had happened to Billy because what they found made no sense.

In the end, they were forced to write a general report which left more questions than answers, and which they were careful to back up with elaborate reasoning and citations from colleagues. Then the little heap of bones was sent up to the village, the reporters were given more generalities than they would have liked, and the funeral finally took place. There was, however, no one left to pay for it, as Billy's remaining relatives were all so distant that no-one wanted to take on the cost. It was paid for somehow in the end, though no-one was quite sure how.

The cottage began to fall into disrepair, and continued that way for many years, only just remaining standing in the winds that drove in from the sea. Inside, it remained just as it had been when Billy was last alive in it, with dirty teacups on the table and the wardrobe full of boxes with dark glass plates. The bird prints had long ago peeled off the wall, but some were still suspended there, hanging by a sinew or a rusty nail, curled and gnarled and turned in on themselves. Curiously, the images remained stark and clear, even though the paper in some cases was so frail it would have crumbled to the touch.

Many years later, Mr. Wilkinson of the City Council, who had retired to the village, decided he would like to buy Billy's cottage and renovate it. It had a wonderful aspect, and views like that could not generally be bought. He faced the problem of who owned it, however, and had to undertake some fairly detailed investigations to locate the nearest relative. It had not really occurred to most people that Billy's cottage belonged to anyone, and it came as a great surprise to the new owner who turned out to be a widow about the same age as Mr. Wilkinson, and Billy was only a peripheral recollection for her.

On learning that she was the owner, she was a little alarmed, as the place was far too much of a responsibility in the state it was, so she was more than willing to sell it to Mr. Wilkinson, provided he was prepared to deal with all the paperwork for her. And so it came about that Mr. Wilkinson discovered Billy's glass plates one day when he started clearing the place out for the builders.

He had known about the photographs, of course. Everyone had. But for the first time, and perhaps because Mr. Wilkinson had time on his hands, he realised that they may have some importance. He took them to the house he was renting in the meantime, and began to take a closer look at them, thinking he might catalogue them and see if the images could be retrieved. Perhaps the local museum might be interested.

Then again, Mr. Wilkinson was rather reluctant to put them into someone else's hands, because there was something about discovering a secret like this which helped to fill his long days. He acquired some digital equipment which he had been advised would reproduce images from glass slides, and he set it up carefully in his living room. Mr. Wilkinson was a man who was used to following instructions, and he set up a methodology for cataloguing the slides as he scanned them onto a screen.

When the first image emerged, he realised that something was not quite right about it, and that perhaps it was over-exposed and needed to be adjusted. There was far too much light. He wondered if he had damaged the image in some way, or if this particular one had simply been over-exposed in the first place, so he tried another from a different box. Each one he tried to scan produced the same result, a mass of white light with something lurking at the back of it which refused to appear, no matter how Mr. Wilkinson adjusted the digital controls. He deduced that the images were too far gone, and that he would just store them away somewhere in case technology should advance to such a stage that it could find the image where he could not.

The next day, he went to finish clearing up in Billy's house, loading things into the skip and removing the stains of a small lifetime so that the house could be retrieved from oblivion. He had made a good purchase. The bedroom was fairly clear now, and it only remained to take down the final peeling bird images so that it would be one less thing for the builders to worry about.

Mr. Wilkinson sat in an old wooden chair to contemplate them for a moment. They were an odd set of pictures for a person like Billy to have had. Owls and geese and creatures which did not, in some cases, seem particularly well proportioned. Mr. Wilkinson knew some of the varieties of bird in the area, but would by no means regard himself as an ornithologist, nor indeed as an amateur birdwatcher. At his age, he was a little too old to assimilate all those lists of names and characteristics and anyway, they seemed a little onerous to him.

As he sat and watched the photographs, he began to feel a little light-headed, and gripped the arms of the chair for a moment, to steady himself. When he looked into the far corner, something moved, and he perceived, or thought he perceived, a large misshapen bird standing staring at him. It had forked feet and a pot belly, and Mr. Wilkinson remembered thinking it reminded him of something from Lewis Carroll.

The creature did not, it seemed, wish him ill, or intend to frighten him, it simply stood there and stared. Mr. Wilkinson, who was a man of solid practicality, sat upright in his chair, but did not feel in any way uncomfortable. He would have liked to have got up and approached the creature, but for some reason the will and the strength had left him, and instead he sat and stared back at the bird in what he considered a form of mutual admiration.

The afternoon wore on, and the light faded, and Mr. Wilkinson and the bird were still there, rooted in each other's gaze. When he did not arrive for his usual evening game of cards with his neighbour, the young men of the village were sent to look for him, and they found a slight, limp body attached to the old chair, with a face full of light and a deep smile but no apparent life.

They called an ambulance and whisked him off to hospital, hoping it was not too late, and he was placed immediately in intensive care after being diagnosed with a heart attack. He stayed there until the doctors felt he was well enough to leave, and was given boxes full of medications with daily instructions, and a note for his G.P. One of his neighbours from the village, who had been coming in every couple of days to cheer him up, arrived with his car to take Mr. Wilkinson home.

"Would you mind very much if we stopped at a florist on the way?" he asked his neighbour. "I'd like to buy some flowers to put somewhere when I get back."

"I hope you're not contemplating going up to that damp house again. The builders will do everything that needs doing. You don't need to do any more, and anyway, if there's anything you need from there, we can get one of the boys to fetch it down."

"No, that's all right," Mr. Wilkinson assured him. "I think I'll just leave whatever's there to the men now, though there were some boxes of old glass slides, and I wouldn't mind having those brought down if anyone were willing to go and fetch them. They'd need a van though. There are quite a few."

They parked at a florist, and Mr. Wilkinson went in and bought a mixture of flowers and some bulbs, then he asked his neighbour to drop him for a moment or two at the cemetery before they went back home. There was something Mr. Wilkinson wanted to do.

His neighbour helped him in through the wrought iron gates of the cemetery, and carried his bunch of flowers and the small bag of bulbs. Mr. Wilkinson, who had not lost his practicality during his weakness, had also thought to buy a small trowel. He instructed the neighbour to place the flowers on the spot where Billy's grave should be and, if he wouldn't mind, to plant the bulbs all over the Johnson plot, even though Billy did not seem to be in it. He then asked his neighbour, who by this time was feeling a little cold and was anxious to get Mr. Wilkinson home, if he would mind filling the empty bulb bag with a little of the earth which had been removed to plant the bulbs.

Only then did Mr. Wilkinson consent to be taken home and installed in front of his television with a hot cup of tea. In the following months, he gradually recovered sufficiently to be able to take morning walks along the cliff top, wrapped up against the spring chill and looking out to sea for something indeterminate. Sometimes his neighbour followed close behind, just to check he was safe and not overexerting himself. He looked a little older now.

One morning, when the signs of summer were beginning to show through, Mr. Wilkinson took the small bag of soil with him which he had brought from the cemetery, scooped it out in small handfuls, and flung it over the cliff top into the spray. He watched it disappear into dust and float away into the ether, and something told him he could now go home. He stood for a few more moments, and watched the gulls and the waves, and then he turned away. He felt, as did most people at that point in life, that he had come full circle.

On the other hand, Billy and his fate remained a mystery, because no-one could quite fathom him or his bones. When the pathologists examined the diminutive body which had blown up on the beach, they did discover one curious thing, however, which they believed somehow significant but which no-one could explain. The bones were not those of an adult, but of a small child, and contained evidence of deep burning, as though they had fallen into a fire. ∎

The Snake Skin

A snake skin is transparent when it dries up, and looks like thin paper, or a brittle shell. It is left there on a sandy track, and the body departs from it into the sand, and becomes something else. Sometimes the snake slides off through a hole in a stone wall, or into the water, and leaves that last life behind it to become part of the sand.

Before I travelled to places where snakes make their tracks on the yellow paths, and before I saw the places where the sun lives, I spent my childhood on an island, a place with an ocean wrapped around it, and dark skies and violent storms in winter. It was a wild rock, appearing and disappearing beneath the waves, because we children strayed often, and were allowed to, so we saw things we perhaps should not have seen under other circumstances.

In summer, when the long days came and I found myself alone with my thoughts on slow evenings which were neither here nor there, I went to the beach and spent time kicking up stones in the sand or running pieces of frosty glass through the salt water to make them shine. I stayed there until the sun had gone down, and then it did not feel such a long road home and I was glad to go inside and sleep.

On these occasions, more than once I found a snake skin, or something like it, but it was bigger and could not have belonged to a snake, nor any reptile. Besides, there were no snakes on the island, nor had there ever been, as far as I knew, and I had never seen one then. Ours was a cold corner with no places for snakes to hide. They were a myth we heard of now and then, and it could not have been otherwise.

I found the skins only because the light of the setting sun made them shine out of the rock and become visible for a few moments before they were shadow again. If I noticed it, which I sometimes did, I went up to take a closer look and touch it to see if it was real. Then, when I reached the rock, especially if it took a long time to climb over to it, the thing was gone, and I realised the light had been playing tricks on my eyes.

At other times, though, it was there, and my hand reached out to see what it felt like. It was never quite the same as the last time and I was never sure whether it would stay or go. As a child, this did not seem an odd state of affairs. On some occasions it was slimy, and on others rough, as I imagined a crocodile to feel. At other times, it was almost furry, like the skin of a mammal or something which preferred the land to the sea. I never thought to move it, because I had no use for it, and I always left it there until the sea or the morning took it away to wherever it had come from. For some reason I never doubted that something had once lived in the skin, but I could not have known that or even deduced it from anything I had learned.

In the winter, when the storms threw things out of the sea with a venom, it never threw up skins and never left anything for long. It was only in summer, for some reason, that these things appeared on the rocks, and then went away again. I was an only child, and was not given to swarming with other boys or making noise or mischief like they did. I could not rise to it, and was not of the ilk. They did not mind it much, and left me to myself for the most part, and my absence meant more of the share of good things for them.

One such summer, when I was about fourteen and growing out of my indulgence, I was aware I would soon be leaving, possibly to work as other men did, and possibly not, but I would not be allowed to spend another summer half way between. I was afraid of what was to come, and did not know what it looked like, or how it would feel, and I wandered through the long evenings kicking up sand on the beach in an effort to forestall it.

It is, I have since discovered, possible to be alone in the world without feeling the worse for it. I do not reject the company of other men or women, but since that summer I have not needed it, nor has it needed me. At times, when I am in the midst of men's ways, living and playing as they are apt to do, I close down a shutter inside myself and join the shadows I became acquainted with before I was forced to become a man.

Only that once, in a moment of brief curiosity, did I transgress where I had not before. Without seeking it, nor indeed wishing it, for I had grown up timid and shelved my curiosity in favour of safe places, I found a skin of a rare quality draped across a rock in a corner of the beach, on the way to the caves and slightly forbidden to the wind. It was smoother than the ones I had seen before, and warmer to the touch, with a whiff of dried herbs or flowers of some description.

I would normally have left it there, as it was of no use to me, and it was too fragile and broken-looking to be of much use to anyone else. On this occasion, however, I took it up in my hands, as it was of uncommon softness and levity, so that I needed to take it away somewhere. More than needing it, I wanted to make sure I could see it. I was not sure what I was going to do with it.

I took it to a shed near our house, and sat outside with it a while to see what it was, or what it might be. It was an animal of some type, maybe of the sea, maybe of the land, I could not tell, because it had dried up and was now paper-thin. It was slightly brittle, and I was careful not to crumple it over much, but it was difficult to hold, even in the light breeze, which caught it and blew it backwards in my hand. When the light faded so that I could no longer see any detail in it, I set it in a box inside the shed and closed the door, so that I could go in to supper and to sleep, and so that I could forget about it until I decided what I needed it for.

That night though, I did not sleep easily. I awoke several times with a sharp gasping for breath which would not ease, and my muscles stretched out into painful spasms to which there seemed to be no end. When I finally slept, I found myself in the middle of a vivid dream.

The Aurora was awake and dancing in my bedroom while I slept, and was playing a sinuous music which bounced off the closed windows and sounded as though it was beginning to cry. It was a sorry sound which could not get out, and which needed to, and I was not prepared to open the window to let it. So it played until it faded out, and sank down into a melancholy which was so doleful it woke me up, and I was glad to be awake because the world I awoke to was more welcoming than sleep.

I went about whatever work I had to do that day, but was not able to shake the memory of the dream, and when the work was done I went to the beach to try and rid myself of it. The beach was long that evening, longer than it usually was, and I walked along it with all the nonchalance I could muster, hoping to make myself tired enough to sleep without dreaming. It was not even sunset, and I resolved to walk until it was.

At the far side of the beach, in the sheltered part where the skin had been draped the previous day, I noticed a slight movement against the light, which was brighter and more blinding at this hour, just before the day left us. I was used to movements like this and paid it no attention, but it shifted again until I had no choice but to approach it, in case I ought to or because I could.

There was nothing on the rock, nor behind it, so I sat there a while and gave it no more thought, though I pondered some things. The sea came and went, as it always did, and nothing else moved because the rocks were fast and there was nothing else. Before long, or only some time, it is hard to say, I felt a hand on my shoulder, from behind like a small bird alighting there, and for some reason, I continued looking out to sea and did not turn around.

At length, I got up to walk away, and saw out of the corner of my eye a shape sitting next to me on the rock, a girl, who was younger, or about my age, and playing with a rock in her hands, turning it over and over without looking at it. I stared at her a while, without her seeing me, because I was ingenuous and at an age where there is no urgency or time, and after a while, she looked up.

You may wonder how I remember it all so vividly, from so long ago, and I can tell you that it is because I am still there, a part of me suspended on that rock in that moment, and whatever followed is peripheral and not part of the same verse. I believe, though I cannot be sure, that the gulls stopped making their noises, and the wind stopped blowing, and I do not know how long I looked into her face before she moved off the rock and sat, instead, cross-legged on the sand.

She asked me - in a voice which was not from the island, but was deeper than her age, and which sat within an accent littered with something foreign and old - whether I would like to take a walk with her, as she was visiting only, and could not stay long. I assumed at this point, with some relief, for we were not used to foreigners on the island, that she was here on the summer boats, and had family on them, waiting for her. And so I was not afraid, as I should have been, because I did not wish to be, and she was a welcome distraction.

She did not tell me her name, because I did not ask it, and it did not seem appropriate to ask, for she began to speak of other things. She asked me first if I knew the fiddle, as she had always longed to play it, and could not learn. I said I did not, because I was not gifted that way, but that I knew many who were, and who entertained us on occasions when they were asked. I said the women did not play, and she should not contemplate it as it would not sit well with the men.

Until this point, I had not looked her in the eye, because my head would not turn upwards, and because boys at that age are awkward. But she bent down slightly and looked at me, and I was startled and turned around, so that I could see she was smiling, and her hair was very long and dark, longer than the hair of any girls I knew, or my cousins' or their friends'. She had dark brown eyes and the skin on her face was either that same colour or burnt long by the sun.

She sat down again on a rock, and motioned that I should do the same. I was in her hands as I could not refuse, and perhaps did not wish to, though the two may be one and the same. She asked me where I would go after the summer, and what I would do. I replied that I did not know, but that the men all went to sea when there was no work on land and there were more mouths than the land could feed, and that I may have to take work on one of the summer boats when they left for wherever they were going to spend the winter.

I did not even know what the boats did, as I had taken no interest in them in case they should spirit me away from the safe haven I had grown into on the island. Other men went, but they were wayward men and returned more wayward still if, indeed, they returned at all. I did not know if my character could sustain such changes with impunity. I was a child with no guidance because it was not spoken of, except in undertones when the wayward men passed by.

The girl, I imagined, was a child of these men who came home when it suited them, and she did not know the things of a settled life, nor did she want them. She asked me then if I had brothers or sisters, and I told her I did not, and that I sometimes wished for them like the other boys. She said she had many, and that they wandered, but were always, somehow, with her, so that she was not alone. When they returned from wherever they went they brought her presents made of things of the sea, and she kept them a while, for as long as they lasted.

I thought her strange, and the things she told me were a little wild and uncanny, so that I listened, but with restraint. This did not seem to worry her at all, and she began to tell me stories of the sea, which, for some reason, I did not find as strange as I found her, and to which I listened with growing interest and a little longing. When she had finished her stories, I began to wonder why she did not leave to go to her wayward family, and her brothers who may or may not have been waiting, but she lingered, and did not appear to be in any hurry.

I, on the other hand, said I would have to go, as it was getting dark, and everyone at home would wonder about me if I did not return soon. I stood up to leave, but she put her hand gently on my elbow and said that, if I left, she would have to go with me. I was stunned for an instant, because I had not expected it, but I also found myself less than unhappy at the prospect, though I did not know what I would do with her or where she would hide amongst the things of our settled life, and I did not think she would stay long. I imagined she would only remain until she had finished the stories she was telling me, and exhausted the questions she asked of me, and until I had given her the answers she craved.

So I led her home, and the journey seemed a little longer than usual. We climbed the sand-banks close to the beach, and then the hill which led to my house, and somewhere along the way, she took my hand and we began to walk together. There are times now when I can still feel her hand in mine through that little eternity, though it cannot, in reality, have been a very long time. It is what I feel when the sun warms my back in the late morning in these hot places where I travel, and it is what sends me to sleep at night when the wind blows too hard on deck or the waves explode under the bows.

Eventually – and by this time it was too soon – we approached the outbuildings close to my house, and I did not know what to do with the girl when we arrived. I could not take her inside, as my family was afraid of the wayward people, and they would have sent her away. She held fast to my hand, and was not afraid as I would have expected her to be, but simply clung to me as though she had become my shadow and I hers. She did not come any closer, though I would have wished it, and her talking ceased as we approached the house.

I became stronger so close to my own world, and needed to protect her from it and it from her, so I took her to a long byre with hay where the cattle slept and told her to wait there for me until morning. It was warm from the cattle's breath and occasional movement, and there was a moon, fully formed, which came through the open holes in the walls. She let go my hand, reluctantly, and let me go into the house, but I did not sleep that night, not even to dream unquiet dreams, and I rose early with remorse and a burning curiosity.

When I looked for her amongst the cattle, she was gone, and I found her wandering around the buildings as though she were looking for something in particular, though I was sure she had never been there before and nothing we had was worth the trouble. At length, she felt me watching her, and turned. She smiled, but this time her smile told me she was concerned about something she could not tell me, and I asked her if she would like me to take her home to the harbour, or to wherever her ship was.

She told me she had no ship, and that her home was not as I imagined, but that she could not return there until I gave her back the part of her I had taken without thinking. I was too young for such stories, and had no idea what she meant, but then she asked me more directly where I had hidden the skin I found on the rock. I had, I confess, forgotten about it, and told her it was rotted and could be of no use to her, but she stopped me in my answer and asked me to give it to her anyway.

Something told me that if I did, I would lose her, and only that once in my life did I wish to hold on to something for ever. Had I known how to refuse, I would have done so, but I could not, for she was crying. I had never seen anyone weep silently before, only in sobs which were aimed at attracting attention. The girl was not begging me, however, with her silent tears. She was crying from a sadness so profound I could not imagine it, and nor could I hold her back.

At length, I shifted from my stupor, and took her hand. I led her to the shed where I had placed the skin, and the brightness returned to her face in an instant. She picked it up and turned it over in her hands to remind herself of something she had lost, and then turned to me to say goodbye. In her dark eyes was a light I have never seen again in all my travels, because it was at once desire which could not be and love which could not stay. Without letting go her skin, she took my hand in hers and placed in it a small piece of frosted beach glass, a muted green with occasional gaps which shone in the last moonlight. Then she asked me to follow her to where she lived, as I was able to make this choice, but she was not.

I allowed her to lead me down to the beach, and we sat for a while on the rock where we had met a small lifetime ago, and we said nothing, though there were words upon words milling around in my head in no particular order. I am not sure how long we waited there, nor indeed why we were waiting when we knew we could not sit there for ever, but after a while she asked me to turn my back and stay away a little, until I heard the sea again.

I had not realised there were no sounds of the sea until she told me, and I did as she asked. The strange silence reigned for some time, and more than once I thought to turn my head but did not, as I trusted her judgement. At length I heard again the sound of the waves, not as they had always been but as though I were hearing them from the inside out, and they were loud and untamed to my ears, which I could not get used to.

I turned, as she had asked me to, towards the sea, and close to the shore I saw the head of a seal dipping below the waves now and then, and at other times holding still in the water. It waited for a long time, and I stood and watched it until my feet began to wander, and I walked towards the edge of the sand where it met the waves. For a while then, I waded through the unfamiliar, each step slower as the water resisted a little, but she did not come closer for all I tried, though I could always see her out of the corner of my eye, and she was smiling.

As my head bowed beneath the waves at first and then a second time, something in me once again became a man, as it would occasionally in years to come, and I reached for the air and gasped in fear. The narrow lane I had been walking which had been calm and a thing of beauty became chaos, and the serene place became mundane. I pushed my body back to the shoreline and, as the beach came closer, my steps became easier, as though I were walking on the tops of the waves.

I sat down in the sand and stayed there for some time, letting the wet particles sift through my fingers, and watching her shadow recede with the dawn and the shifting light. I did not move for many hours, and eventually men were sent to find me and take me back to the world they lived in, but for many days I was unable to rise from my bed or my stupor, and they tell me I wept.

One day I awoke in a clearer state of mind, and announced to the people around me that I was going away. They were not surprised, and I think had seen it coming a long time before I had, and they helped me pack whatever I would need. I walked down to the harbour where the last of the summer boats lay, and I asked in one after another if they had a place for me. I took the first one that was willing to have me, and did not look back, nor did anyone try to make me.

In the years to come, I wandered the earth, moving from ship to ship and from land to land, and nowhere could hold me down for long. The work kept me alive, and I was a good hand, always there when I was needed because I was always escaping distraction, for fear it would lead me away. Sometimes though, at nights, when the sun was setting, if there was nothing to do, and especially if we were in northern waters which were quiet for a while, I watched the waves from the deck the whole night long. On such occasions I asked always that a man stay with me, one who could be trusted not to turn away for a moment, for I knew I could not help myself.

When we are landbound for a few days, I walk as far as I can inland, and stay there until the ship sails or the sea calls me back again, because I am afraid that, if I do not, I will lose my place in the world of men. I know that one day I will have to leave, but I still do not know how, for all I am weak and would let myself be taken by any wave that would have me.

When I have docked somewhere and left the men behind and set off on foot into some interior I know or know not, and when the sun is about to go behind the stone walls and cobbled-up wooden gates in some place where there is no rain, I see a smile lingering in the snakeskins in the sand and I start to follow, because I am willing, and because I have nowhere else to go. Even in places where there is no day in winter and no night in summer I have to find a straight line to walk, otherwise I cannot predict the consequences.

Whenever I return to the island – though it is no longer home, only a stopping place amongst many – I see her sometimes, close to the shore, always alone. She waits a while for me to sit down in the sand and watch, as she knows I will, and then she lifts her head and I hear her, though I am not sure how. She never has a mate, unless he is somewhere hidden, and she never has pups, because I think that is where I deprived her, and she would tell me if she could that it was my choice, not hers. She does not think less of me for it, but sometimes weeps for what might have been. Each time, I stop only a little short of following her. ■

The Poems of Ossian

I remember only the rain that year, the torrents of it and the drizzle. Perhaps it would have been different if it had not been raining. Then again, different may have been even worse. In ten months it did not stop raining, and everyone's feet were wrinkled with sitting inside wet shoes which never quite dried. Even at night, it rained.

I was a distracted student that year, my second at university. I had realised I did not particularly want to be there, and was not ready. The world was waiting elsewhere and my head turned to it each time it called, so that I could not be tempted to stay and be part of the lecture hall or the tutorial. Besides, the true depths of academia escaped me until it was far too late.

On the other hand, perhaps my lack of focus was what led me to the book and its consequences, and perhaps, after all, that is what led me here. I have always loved books for their content, and how they feel in my hand and seem to the eye. It has never particularly mattered to me whether they are perfect or imperfect, battered or whole, or whether they are valuable and worth money in the auction room. Despite all my distractions, I have always loved the books.

Our campus was cobbled together in those days, whole departments housed in decrepit buildings on its margins, and something of an air of mystery still hovered over academia. Ours was a detached Edwardian affair, which had once been a family home, perched on a small promontory, quite on its own and always a little crooked in its aspect. The rain hit it sideways, at odd angles, because it sat at an odd angle itself. The outside woodwork was painted black, and when I think about it, that should have made it look drab and undistinguished but, as though it were bound to lean, it never seemed to be quite of this world, and stood out in rather stark outline on the campus horizon. The building has now long since been demolished, and the department re-housed in a steel-rimmed edifice with central heating and safety regulations. The last time I visited, briefly, I was disoriented and had trouble finding its soul.

When you climbed the steps to the front door of the old house and entered the building, there was never anyone there. It did not matter what time of day it was, I could walk through the front door, deposit my umbrella and wet coat where everyone else had left theirs, and be reasonably sure of meeting no-one until I went further inside. The entrance to the remainder of the department was through what appeared to be a cupboard door, and in later years – but not then – I recalled C.S. Lewis when I thought of it.

It led down some broken wooden stairs into a basement where there was a small departmental library and the office of a remarkable professor whose story would not lie down, nor would it be told. The remainder of the staff lived upstairs and had the lion's share of the daylight, what little there was that year. I imagine I must have had classes upstairs too, but I only remember the ones in the basement.

The professor was, as I recall, half real and half invented, not because he had devised a mythical persona for himself, but because people had invented one for him. I have since thought that this was partly because he did not rank conspicuously in the cut-throat world of academic hierarchies and partly, I am quite sure, because he told stories. In truth, the stories were all quite real, but in those days, no-one knew whom to believe, and we had to pass exams, when all was said and done.

I was assigned to him because of the subject of my undergraduate dissertation, which was not considered to be on a particularly relevant theme. I was on the point of giving it up and agreeing to a more mainstream line, because I had no confidence or ammunition, when the professor himself stepped in, listening in the wings, and said he would be delighted to take it on. What is more, it was – he seemed to think – high time he was assigned an undergraduate.

It was at this point that the dissertation became at once a responsibility and a somewhat tentative journey, because I had chosen it and it could no longer be someone else's fault. I walked out into the drizzle that day, forgetting my umbrella because I had entered for the first time into something more important, which was a distraction of a different kind.

Perhaps there is still a place where education is allowed to be a mystery and where it has not yet become a series of lists and packages and training plans. If there is, it can, of course, lead to madness, but for those who can stand back a little and have the good fortune to be assigned teachers of a different calibre, it may become the cornerstone of a vast infinity which does not fade with age or time.

The dissertation gave me a new lease of life, and I began to take more care of myself and my work. I attended lectures, even when I was ill, which I often was in the extended dampness and its mouldy residue. I did not sleep well, because I was generally cold, and developed a skin disease which I was told originated somewhere in my own head, so I let it fester because it was my fault.

I lived, when I could, in the small departmental library in the basement, even though the most extensive range of books was in the vast modern building with sharp edges where there were proper procedures and lifts, and staff to steer you through the set themes and tasks. I must have thought, even then, that a guided path is not particularly worth following, as it is finite, a cul-de-sac with instructions.

I felt comfortable in the small library, and knew almost every book in it and where it sat. For all its size, it did not have limits like the main places of study, and appeared expansive in its scope because it was only ever meant to be a starting place. The big library had all the answers, stacked neatly and arranged in such a way that you could not fail, like painting by numbers or a manual on how to play the violin. There was scant exchange between the book and the reader, except to extract the products in their little boxes. The lists and the librarians were always there to remind you if you strayed a little off the path. Besides, it always felt very slightly cold in there, despite the regulation heating, a fact I attributed to its high ceilings and empty spaces.

The small library had old-fashioned heaters which had to be switched on when someone opened up in the mornings, so that, if you had been drenched to the bone by the rain, and even if you had left your outer coats at the door upstairs, steam rose through the room for a while, until it settled. It probably accounts for why some of the books had turned-up leaves, but it meant you could taste the tales the author was still trying to tell across the generations.

When the whole class had an assignment, no-one could ever find the recommended books in their places because the professor involved had always taken them out for his own use, forgotten to return them, and had to be reminded before anyone else could borrow them. I was never annoyed by this like the other students, because it gave me an excuse to spend time lost in the books for my dissertation which, by the very nature of the theme, no-one else ever took out, and they were hidden in parts of the library which gathered dust.

Whenever I could, I stayed in the library until it closed, because it was preferable to the rain and to the damp quarters I lived in, and to the skin disease which kept me awake at nights. Then, and later, I have often been a victim of misunderstanding, and I rather fear the staff thought my inertia and sleepiness in lectures was due to long nights on the town and a lack of study or responsibility. I was, and still am, too naïve in thinking the best of people, and did not defend myself until the impression was carved in stone. Perhaps that is for the best, after all.

At times, I was the only person left in there, except for the duty librarian, usually a post-graduate or someone who would have been in the library anyway, and it was not impinging on their need to be somewhere else. The books I remember most were those written in the 1920s and '30s, in the heyday of exploration to far-flung places where the culture was of a different kind. It was between the wars, when people still remembered the horror sufficiently to be able to enjoy the respite in case it came back, as it always did.

And then there were the classics, not the ones written by the authors we studied, but the ones they themselves had read, and which fired their imagination until they, too, wrote. Some of these books had broken spines and pages missing because, sometime long ago, they had been read, and read, and read. Some of them had been discredited, and so were no longer taken seriously, but they had still told stories which fuelled the words of the great writers to come, until the old volumes became secrets again. I especially loved the books which had been forgotten.

Opposite the campus, a long walk in the rain from the department, was a second hand bookshop. It was like most shops of its kind even today, housed in a semi-derelict building which was almost as battered as some of the books it sold, and it had old electric heaters, fire hazards in waiting, as though the books were always perched on the margins of extinction. For this, they were always a pleasure, as they were transitory.

When the library had closed, sometimes the bookshop was still open for half an hour or so, and I could never pass without going in, no matter how pressing the evening was, or how tired I might be. I never went to any stack in particular, because I was never looking for anything determinate, and that day I landed in a corner of ancient-looking books which seemed almost ready to disintegrate.

There was the usual Shelley and Walter Scott, and one or two commentaries which someone had written in a dark study somewhere, and published so that they were not forgotten or because they believed them worthwhile. Wedged in amongst these pamphlets and stories and poems was a small brown and gilt-covered volume of the type common between the 18th and 19th centuries, and which had no doubt been carried around by someone to read in dull moments. I took the book from the shelf, and had to catch its cover, as it was loose and almost fell to the ground.

The inside cover read, in a flowery sort of script, "The Poems of Ossian, translated by James MacPherson, in two volumes," and its date was given as 1807. The opening pages were filled with fading illustrations of men and gods and heroes in dark skies, poised to leap from the edge of the page should anyone question their authenticity. The little volume had been kept well, however, apart from its falling cover and its yellow edges, and the pages were strong and stark, despite the many hands they had seen. I could not see much more, because the light in the shop was poor, and made worse by the gloom outside in the damp twilight.

I had no money to speak of, but used my bus fare home to buy the book, and held it inside my coat to keep the rain from it. It was a long walk to the cold place where I lived, and all the libraries were closed, so I had no choice but to continue. At length I arrived with Ossian tucked under my wet clothes, and I switched on the old electric fire which filled the room with steam and vapour.

Eventually I warmed up sufficiently to think clearly.

I did not eat well that year, because I could never think of anything I would like to eat, and because, when I did, I could not be bothered to go out and find it. I often went straight to bed to sleep when I came in from the library, knowing that I would not sleep long, and would find myself waking up in the middle of the night and retrieving some assignment or work which needed to be completed. It is the only time I have been nocturnal, and it did not sit well with me.

On this occasion, though, I took a hot cup of tea and opened the brown package containing Ossian, and leafed through the pages, being careful not to tear any which time had stuck together. Only at this point was I struck by the date and the title wording. I knew that Goethe and the great poets of central Europe had been greatly taken with MacPherson's discovery of the ancient poems, and it had given focus to their own imagination so that whole movements were born which history would favour and remember. Ossian itself had faded into obscurity when it was suspected not to have been the translation of an original manuscript, but rather a story patched together by MacPherson himself, and therefore not to be entertained.

The same people who had embraced the stories with open arms, and who had exchanged parts of their daily lives for the labyrinths of the ancient world, the same people whose imaginations had been awoken by the words, turned away from the little book and were ashamed to have been deceived. It was denounced with ugly names which should never be used to describe books, but by this time its words had already found their way into the great works of the future, and it lived on a little through them, because it told stories that people, in truth, wanted to hear.

When I looked again at the date, I realised that this volume had been published when MacPherson still had enough credibility to be considered its translator, and Oisín himself the author. It was published, and bought, and read at a time when some people still believed in it, and before it had been entirely rejected by those whose only and greatest fear was being deceived. Somehow it had survived, and passed from shelf to shelf, derided a little, but someone did not quite have the heart to discard it completely. In amongst its pages, the stories were there still, and did not fade with the paper.

I took the book to a relevant professor, who was intrigued by it and did not belittle my enthusiasm, but he had other things on his mind. He also said it was a shame that I had only found volume one, and that it might be worth looking for its partner. This was the first time I had properly taken note of the fact that it was only one of two volumes. For a moment, I was gripped by the same absurd thoughts as must have passed through the minds of readers when they were told that MacPherson had deceived them, and I thought perhaps the book's value could be salvaged if it were reunited with volume two.

I rushed out to the bookshop and missed a lecture so that I could rummage through the shelves to find Ossian's other part. I tried the shelf where I had found it, but the nature of second hand bookshops does not generally lend itself to the instant location of titles, nor should it. Shelley and Scott still prevailed, as they often do, but Ossian was nowhere to be found. I tried other shelves with works from the same period, and then shelves with similar themes, and then ones with nothing in common at all. Finally, I asked the assistant, who was reading a comic close to the window to attract whatever daylight was available, but he was surly and just shook his head. I did not think he really wanted to be there.

Somehow my own credibility had diminished with the value of the book. I was a little down-trodden by it all, and put the little book to one side for a while. I took it out occasionally because, despite it all, it had something of a white light inside it, one which would not fade, because it was still trying to tell a story. I was too young, and allowed myself to be overruled by the greater confidence of others.

I continued writing my dissertation, delving in and out of the books in the small library, guided here and there along the road by the professor who hid in the cupboard in the basement and who also had stories which would not be told. He had tried to publish his own work with little success, partly because the subject was one which was not widely spoken of or well received in an academic world which preferred its people to walk in straight lines.

When I presented him with the finished work, he was pleased with it, and we made some adjustments here and there until it was ready. I had written about a place and a people who were familiar to him, and who did not see things in quite the same way as the world I lived in. Perhaps just a little, this had fed some of the stories he had half given up and which had been consigned to the dusty end of the library.

I finished my degree, a fact which surprised me as much as my teachers, not because I was not diligent, but because I never quite recovered my spirit after that year, and I hoped only to leave and go away to somewhere that could not haunt me. I wandered off, after that, into the everyday world, trying to hold myself down in it and to follow the rules I was led to believe would keep me safe. I could never quite find my place in it, though, in the daily lives with their rates of success and failure, and mostly I did not try very hard.

Many years later, I was living in a small place where people did not think far beyond their own boundaries, and as I was rearranging the bookshelves one day, I came across the little book of

Ossian. It was a sad time, that year too, and I sat down on the floor to open the book with tears streaming down my face for something I had lost and could not quite define. I opened the pages and began to look at the words, and realised that I had never actually read the book as I had been disheartened after I had been unable to locate the second volume.

I had a good friend in those days, someone who, like me, could not quite find her place between the tram tracks, but who had tried hard to do so for fear of offending. In her old age, she told me stories which gave me back some of the spirit I had lost in making my way through the arbitrary world of offices and workplaces.

My friend had a very particular talent for finding books, long before the Internet, in the days when rare books were still hard to find, and locating them was an art and a pleasure, and even a mystery. I had never really spoken to her of Ossian, nor of my undergraduate days, but I skirted around the subject in one way or another. We spoke about the poets sometimes, and about the mysteries of the universe, and this whiled away dark afternoons in winter when the wind blew and the light was gone, and with the stories, I came to smile again.

One Christmas, only a year before she died, she presented me with a package to take home and place under the Christmas tree. In it, she said, were a few things for me and my family – just something to open on Christmas morning. I thanked her and handed her my own contribution to her Christmas Day. She knew, I think, that she might not see another one, but I did not, and so this was just another occasion amongst many and I still believed the world went on for ever in its humdrum way.

I found time that night when everyone had gone to bed to take out the little volume of Ossian and read aloud to myself:

"Once we wrestled on Malmor..."

It was full of blood and deeds and dynasties, and I could not quite see where Goethe had found his inspiration, for it seemed a little contrived. I also noticed for the first time that the pages were not in order, or that some were missing, even though it was an original volume, so that the page numbers occasionally did not correlate, and the words did not follow on or make sense.

I was, however, taken with the book, and especially its odd page numbering, and took to reading it more often, when I needed to find a space away from the daily world and its expectations. At length, an antique dealer set up in the town, not far from our tiny place, and on a whim I took Ossian to him one day and said, "I wonder if you know where I might find the second volume to this?" I added, sheepishly, that I thought it might be quite valuable if we could find it, because I had come to crave credibility from the world where things are considered to have monetary value.

The owner took one look at the book, with a little disdain I detected, and turned it over in his hands clumsily and without interest, so that the front cover fell to the floor. "I wouldn't bother," he said. "It's falling apart. If it had been in a better state of preservation, then maybe – but it's really worth nothing at all. You do know it was a fake?"

Something snapped inside me, and all the things which had ever gone wrong in my life, and all the times I had never spoken my mind, descended upon me in a single moment and I began to cry. I apologised, and said, "But look at the date. It was published when some people still thought MacPherson had translated it from an original manuscript, and think of all the great writers who read it and were spurred on by it, and all the great literature that was written as a result." I was trying not to sound too absurd or unreasonable, but was aware that I would probably never be taken seriously again. The town was a small place, not much bigger than the hidden corner I lived in, and people worked hard for their credibility and hid their fears and weaknesses so as not to lose it.

The man handed me a tissue from a box on his desk, but wiping away the tears did not stop them. "I'm sorry," the man said, rather embarrassed in case anyone else should walk in. "It's a sad fact, I'm afraid. The book is just an imperfection – it's falling apart and its pages are not even consecutive. Look – it can't really have been worth much when it was printed, and I'm sorry to say it could be worth even less today in real terms. The other volume was probably thrown away years ago by someone who discovered its defects, and this one probably ended up in some second hand bookshop as part of a job lot after someone died and their house was cleared out. Sorry I can't help you, but I do think it's best you know."

I took Ossian Volume One back to my car, placed it on the seat beside me, and attempted to calm myself before I drove home. It was raining, and a few drops had found their way onto the cover of the book, the back cover which was still intact, and which was holding the volume together. I picked it up again and wiped off the drop of water as though it were a tear and the book were crying, and I opened it up and began to read:

"Cuthullin sat by Tura's wall: by the tree of the rustling sound. His spear leaning against a rock."

And I began to hear, with all its imperfections and lack of syntax, and page numbers in the wrong order, what Goethe must have heard, and the words sounded like disjointed poetry again, two hundred years later. When I had finished reading, I took the little book and held it between the palms of my hands to keep it warm, and then

I wrapped it up in a glove and took it home. I opened it when I felt like it, not every day, but whenever I wanted to hear the words the same way as I had heard them in the car that day, and it sat in pride of place above all the perfect ones and the ones whose words had not aged or become discredited. I think I had always loved it the best, but had never really discovered how to read it.

A few weeks later, on Christmas Day, when my children had opened all their presents and I was able to sit down in peace for a few moments, I took the parcel my friend had given me and opened it up. It contained a few things for my children, Christmas things which were meant and received well. Then I came to my presents, and I opened the first one slowly, because there was no urgency, and because the day had a long way to go.

Inside was a book by my old professor at the university, and I smiled. He had finally managed to publish his ideas, just as they were and not changed to fit any straight lines or anyone's prejudices. It had taken him 20 years, but he had not compromised along the way, thinking, no doubt, that there was no point in publishing lies or half truths, or someone else's thoughts. For some reason, I was also very slightly proud of myself when I saw the cover, and I smiled again, because I had never spoken to my friend of the professor, and did not know how she could have guessed.

I turned to the second parcel, and pulled open the wrapping, which stuck a little because it was tightly bound. The contents were moving a little inside, as though they were fragile, and I realised I should be careful. A small brown volume emerged from the package, and I looked at the spine to see what it was, but the spine was missing. The cover, too, was loose, and hanging by a thread, so I opened it carefully and tried not to disturb the pages too much. The book, however, opened of its own accord, and the pages inside were not faded as I had expected. They were not even yellow, but were cut a little roughly at the edges, and opened at the title page.

The Poems of Ossian, translated by James MacPherson, in two volumes. 1807.

Volume Two.

After my friend died, the following year, I took out the two volumes to show them to a visitor, and to point out how much I loved the anomalies like the pages which did not correlate or quite follow on from one another. The little volumes of Ossian, however, had shifted slightly into something I still do not understand, and do not wish to, because it is as it should be. The pages of both of them had become consecutive, and the poetry aligned with itself, so that it had reached its own level. And so they remain yet. ∎

The Long Wait

Waiting is easy, or hard, depending on how you look at it. It can be a blessing when nothing else can ease the pain, or it can be a black hole from which you never return the same person. Whichever way it goes, it will change someone inside, though it may not appear so, and sometimes it makes them well.

We waited for seven months and six days. We waited and watched until our eyes and heads were sore with waiting, and finally we began to drift away, one by one. My younger brother went home first. We saw him less and less, as the world reclaimed him and put him to good use. Then my younger sister, as she found her way back into her own family and sat alongside her children once again. Only my older sister and I were still there to watch my mother return to us as though she had never been away. One morning, after she had been in that other place for seven months and six days, she walked back out onto the stones in front of our old porch and smiled a quiet smile which told us we had not been waiting in vain.

By the time the waiting came to an end I had finally discovered where my mother went on her journeys, and slowly she passed me the key to the door where they began. It helped me to find relief from the weary obligations of the mildly successful normality I had left behind in the boxed places of the world. I am happy to say I have learned how to live comfortably in this limbo, safer in the striding of long days and steep shadows than in the certainties men like to create for themselves.

My sister's voice on the answer phone was the first to tell me about my mother's illness. I had returned home late from one of those interminable meetings which should never take place because they achieve nothing except to reassure the participants that they are residing safely inside the mediocre. I was weary because I increasingly found the world did not have a place for me and I was becoming invisible within its narrow confines, yet I could not bring myself to step away from it.

That evening I gave in to the weariness and intended to have an early night, to wash myself clean of the day and its vagaries. I should not have checked the phone messages. On previous evenings, I had toyed with the idea of disconnecting the phone, or at least the answer phone. People rarely phoned me to exchange pleasantries, but usually to pass on to me work they found boring or too difficult. Sometimes it was paperwork the squadrons of faceless public sector workers were drowning in by 4pm on a Friday afternoon, so they passed it on to someone else in an effort to tidy their weekend. I am happy to say I no longer check messages and have dispensed with the answer phone.

On this occasion, though, my sister's voice intruded into my kitchen with a note of desperation. We did not speak often, and I did not at first make the mental shift between my world and hers.

"I think you'd better come home. Mum's not good. Just come. You'll see when you get here."

My first thoughts were not, lamentably, for my mother or what might ail her, or how long, or how soon. I did not, in fact, think about my mother at all. My family was like that. We watched each other from afar and smiled across distances, but we did not gush or climb into each other's lives where we would fester. We saw photographs of one another standing on long roads and heard the sound of each other's voices down the occasional phone line, and watched images on screens which played back smiles on our faces so that we had no need for words. That was the way we stayed together when so many fell apart from needing too much.

My fears were not for my mother, who was brave in a way the world does not understand, but for myself. I was afraid to go back to the place where I had become a man, because I understood the dangers of going backwards. I would have to step outside the narcotic straight lines I had built to help me live the way everyone wanted, and it was a journey I had avoided making for as long as I could remember or wished to contemplate.

The jigsaw puzzle of my childhood was a mish-mash of what was real and what I liked to think, some of it music and some of it noise. My sister liked to reminisce on the few occasions I saw her, because we were the only ones left who thought about it at all, but I shied away and changed the subject in case it came close to the truth. The memory of my childhood was doing no harm as a sleeping myth. The news of my mother's illness, however, forced me out of my cushioned

172

existence. I was confronted by mirrors of responsibility, and I knew I could not leave my sister to deal with it on her own. The world of architecture would have to do without me for a while.

It was a boxed sort of world I had chosen as a profession, with its angles and corners, but the only place where I had safely been able to find art. Had I become an artist, I would probably have succumbed to madness, but in the lines of buildings which joined opposite spaces together, I had found a tolerable level for my wayward talents.

I followed the rules, but in my spare time when no-one was there to see me, I bent them to build curves where the straight lines used to be. I amused myself by designing structures no-one would ever build because they could not be made to serve. My passion was follies, the bizarre structures of the 18th and 19th centuries, erected as an antidote to the mundane. They were where the rich men who still had imagination kept the souls of their big houses because it was where nobody thought to look. They built towers and pavilions, temples with faces and even lakes where Paracelsus was alive and well, upside down.

These buildings stood out on the landscape in their incongruity, and from the tops of their hills they smiled down and invited us to join them in the in-between, if we dared. The world of architecture did not, on the whole, appreciate follies because they were seen as twisted or bent examples of their art, but they are my passion because they will not lie down to be drawn.

My excursions to these anomalies were journeys into the comfortable tranquillity of chaos, and were only possible because I had not burdened myself with a wife and children which, I felt sure, came with the inescapable social obligation of theme parks. I felt quite at home in the bizarre world of irregular buildings, but quietly, without the need to put them to use. I had built for myself a curious network of comfort zones which are triggered by seeing a winding road which does not end, or when I hear Italian spoken, or feel the sun on my back. In short, I developed a strategy for surviving in a world where I do not belong.

So I was reluctant to stray backwards into my childhood, to step back onto that island perched between the sea and the sky where people live according to their own rules and where survival is a mental, rather than a physical thing. If you are able to fit in, you survive, and if you do not, for whatever reason, no amount of trying will suffice, and you eventually have to go away for your own good.

I absentmindedly phoned a message in to my work explaining the situation, and packed a bag which consisted of only a few clothes alongside many more items which were of greater importance to me, such as a small kaleidoscope in a travelling box and a guide to the great follies at Sintra. Telephones, mobile or otherwise, did not sit well with me, and rather than phoning to book a flight, I preferred to take a train to the airport on the off chance that there would be a place. I did not like organised journeys and this was a small act of defiance.

The train journey was not a long one, but I always relished it. Whatever I had with me to pass the time, like a book, was really only my attempt to bow to the norms of the acceptable traveller, and it very quickly gave way to watching whatever was flying past outside the window. Staring through the glass of a train window is, in

my opinion, an art, and should never be underes-
timated.

On such journeys I watch with amusement the
young men who cannot travel alone, even if their
companion is only the music coming from the
wires in their ears or the games on the machine
their fingers twitch over, as though the little
boxes connect them to some nebulous Big Brother
out there in the city. I have never been able to do
that. I revert each time to the landscape outside
the train window, no matter how bland, whether
it is a city or a field. My train windows are a blur
of images containing other people's back gardens,
with whatever they have collected together in
their days, the places where they think their lives
are not being watched. I do not believe I have
ever found a journey boring, only the destination.

And so, for this reason, I am always pleased
when the train journey ends in an airport, so that
it can go on in some other form. I love airports,
and would have no trouble spending weeks in
one, watching the journeys go by. They are invariably spacious places with light and warmth, and
are built to encourage dreams. Waiting in an
airport is always a pleasure. I find myself a seat

by one of the large windows, and watch the dreams come and go.

I have always found that when I do not need something or have an urgency for it, it will always turn up of its own accord. I was half hoping there were no planes to the islands, or no spaces on them, because then I could delay, but there were two places left, and the daily side of me told me I must take one of them. As soon as we took off the anticlimax began, staved off only by the clouds. When all the other passengers stopped looking out of the window because of the cloud cover, I sat back and enjoyed a long voyage through the ether.

We touched down before sunset, if indeed you could call it that amongst the dark grey. A wind was threatening, as it often was, and I picked up a hire car and drove away to catch the ferry to the remoter island where I was born. Having got this close, a familiar urgency set in to get home before the storm gathered, otherwise the ferry would not run and I would be stuck for an expensive few days in a Bed and Breakfast, a forced wait with no solace, and neither here nor there.

The ferry ran, however, and bounced its way across the Sound for nearly half an hour until we reached the other shore. It would probably not do any more runs that day as the weather was worsening. I was not like the other men born on the island, hardened to the sea, and I arrived looking pale and wishing I had not eaten anything on the plane. I drove slowly down the long, winding road to the other side.

Only when I approached my sister's house did I give a thought to trepidation. I had successfully staved off any speculation about what my mother's illness might mean for us, but deep down inside me I could hazard a reluctant guess as to how I would find her. I was greeted at the door by my younger brother who had arrived before me, because he had only had to come from the town on the main island. It was starting to rain.

I deposited my luggage in a corner of the kitchen and began to make myself a cup of tea. This was the house where I had grown up, and I knew how to make myself at home in it. While the water boiled, my brother appraised me of the situation. My mother, it seemed, had become unresponsive, and would speak to no-one. She went about her daily life as normal, but was given to staring into the distance as though something there had caught her attention and held her gaze in it without letting go. At the moment, my brother said, she was sleeping and probably would not be able to see me until morning.

I tried to picture how she might look and whether she would recognise me. I could picture her staring into the ether. It had happened once before, I remembered, when we were children, but my memory of it had merged into the mundane, as it does until children grow up and start questioning whether their lives are different from other people's.

My father had died when I was five, one night while we were asleep. My mother did not see it coming, but my father did. In his last few months he had said things to prepare us, but we were not listening because we did not understand, and my mother was not listening because she did not want to hear. They had married late in life, and in doing so, had become indispensable to one another. Overnight, he disappeared. There was no trace of him when I came downstairs in the morning, and his armchair was empty. No-one dared sit in it again, and after that my life changed.

My mother sat and rocked herself back and forth until the women came and dragged her back to work, to make her blood flow again, because they were afraid they might lose her too. They took her to the cattle and made her herd them back and forth to the fields to give her soul back the rhythm that at least gave it the semblance of life. By the time my mother finally slid out of her grief, we children were wild and lost and wandered the island to avoid all forms of belonging.

I could still see my mother's face during that time, calm and peaceful and not betraying the slightest fear, but her eyes were trained on the horizon and did not move from it from one day to the next. We could not see what she was looking at, nor would we have been able to had we really tried, because we did not have the key to where she went. We did not have the key because we were afraid and listless, and were trying too hard to bring her back.

Unlike my brother, who was younger than me and did not remember this incident, I knew there was nothing we could do until it was over. She would come when she was ready, but that was not what the world expected of us. We would need to be seen to rush around in circles, busying ourselves with the semblance of making progress, as this is how the world judges whether or not people care. I have never understood why we could not be allowed to care as we saw fit. After all, we were the ones having to cope with it.

The medical authorities were consulted but had no answers except to pass her on through an endless labyrinth of experts who fished about for a name, had tests done and reluctantly admitted that my mother's condition could not be defined by the results. Perhaps it was dementia, but it was too early to tell. My mother was not disoriented and did not do strange things like putting her money down the toilet or salt in her tea. She had no gradual slide into peculiarity. My mother had just, quite suddenly one day, gone on a long journey where we could not go. She stared out to sea as though she were watching a film on the waves, and seemed perfectly happy doing so.

Before the results came in, the local doctor was uneasy at the thought of having a possible dementia case on her hands, and suggested we move my mother out to the town, where one of us could take care of her. We were not sure which universe the doctor was living in, but it must have been one where people did not have to work for a living because any attempt at explaining why this might be difficult seemed to turn in on us to make us feel guilty of neglect. Whichever way I looked at it, I could guess better than anyone where my mother had gone, and was prepared to wait patiently for her to come back. She was not doing any harm where she was, except to frighten everyone who could not find a satisfactory solution.

Children with my mother's symptoms, I later realised, often become educational experiments, bouncing back and forth between people's theses and theories and carrying labels through life to prevent them from being bullied. For us, though, there was only speculation. My sister eventually came down from watching my mother where she spent her days. She also knew, I feel sure, that my mother was safe and that we did not need to keep watch, but my sister sat so uncomfortably between what she knew and what people expected of her that she was unable to make lateral decisions for herself for fear of being misjudged.

She told us how my mother had disappeared from her one day. She had not physically gone anywhere, but her eyes had trained on the horizon and would not leave it. She had been standing in the field next to the house, the one that overlooks the sea, and had looked up, across at the headland on the opposite side of the bay. A smile had slowly covered her face, a strange beam which made her whole face light up, and she dropped the hoe she was using and sat down in the field to watch the thing across the bay which was making her so happy.

My sister had tried first of all to see what it was, but there was nothing unusual, just the headland and the gulls circling over it. Sometimes, after it rained and the sun came out, excess water fell off the edge of the cliff like a cataract or a beam of light, but on this occasion there was nothing of that ilk at all. My sister had taken my mother indoors. She had not resisted, but went willingly, and climbed into bed. In the mornings after that, she got up and did some chores mechanically, but would not talk. All that apparently remained of my mother was a serene smile which lived on without her.

For the time being, it seemed, we would just have to wait, to sit it out. When I came down to the kitchen in the morning, my mother was already about, collecting eggs from the henhouse. She came and went, smiled when she saw me and wandered past as though I had been there all the time. She said nothing, but it was as if she were saying to me, "I've no idea who you are, but you seem a nice sort of person, so I'll just go about my business and you go about yours." The world in which my mother was living was one in which she clearly felt more comfortable than I did in mine.

My sisters and brothers and I shared out what had to be done, and speculated about what might come next. My sister, understandably, did not wish to be left with the problem by herself. Like me, she had never married, and had stayed with my mother to run the farm, but with the latest developments she felt the world closing in on her, and did not want to bear the burden alone. She saw it going on for ever, and realised she was trapped.

So we discussed whether my mother should be moved to a place where help was readily available, the town maybe, or at least nearer to where we could all take turns. But we were not there yet. We had not yet reached the state of desperation where we had to do that, and we were still able to consider alternatives. Had we known how long it would go on we would not, I think, have been so careful.

Part of it was guilt. We all knew how people would view us for taking the easy way out. That was not the way it was done. The social rules did get changed sometimes, if you were self confident enough to do what you thought best instead of succumbing to how you were expected to think, but none of us in my family ever had much self-confidence. We knew that, no matter how hard we tried to make decisions for ourselves, everyone else could still make it hurt.

It was the same when someone died. The person was dead and there was not much you could do about that, but the eyes of the men and women of the island were watching to see that the family members grieved correctly. I was not given to this, and could not see the point. As a child I had been close to an uncle, but when he died, I did not come to his funeral. Instead, I went to a lake I knew near my house in the city, one he had enjoyed when he had visited me as an old man, and I sat there to be with him while he prepared to leave us forever, the tears rolling down my cheeks. On the island, where he was being buried, I was, I understand, more of a topic of whispered conversation than the old man himself, but I maintained my right to grieve as I wished, for I had known him best.

For the island community, our epitaphs are determined by how many people attend our funeral. It's a little like an exam where you have one chance to get a good mark. I often thought of the quiet people, the silent old men who came and went on this earth with no-one but themselves to judge, and I pictured them floating away unnoticed, but I could not imagine they were any the worse for it in eternity. How strangely men and women of the world like to comfort themselves with numbers.

My mother was not dying. I knew that instinctively, but the doctor clucked around in her characteristically pessimistic way, telling us we should be prepared for the worst, and needed to give some thought to how we were going to deal with it. If we were lucky, she said, it would be quick, but it could take years and we needed to think carefully so that they could put into motion whatever solution we decided upon.

Her assumption was that we would opt for care, and it was a very tempting option. We were being presented with urgent choices. Decide now or forever hold your peace. "Later on," the doctor said, "it may not be possible. She may be too ill for anywhere to consider taking her in." To the credit of my family, those of us who were left to decide sat and disentangled the options in our own way, and for once closed the doors on the world and the pressure it put us under. We shut out the people peering around the door as much as we shut out the authorities, not for fear of how they might judge us, but for fear that we would not have the confidence to overrule them.

That weekend, we talked endlessly, winding in and out of the options and discussing almost anything except my mother. Discussing my mother would, to be fair, have been counterproductive. My brothers and sisters wanted to focus on the practicalities of how we were going to manage her for however long it took. Throughout it all I knew my mother would return one day. I cannot recall how I knew, whether it was because I had seen her return before and remembered it vividly, or whether, without realising it, I had been to that place myself, and had no fear of it. I have always been more afraid of the world itself than of what lay behind it.

To everyone's credit, they agreed that her recovery was a possibility, and that sending her away might jeopardise it more than if we kept her with us. My older sister would only consent to this if she were not left alone with the daily coping, and that was where the greatest decision arose. We all agreed that my mother herself presented no difficulties. She wandered blissfully through the days from wherever she was, but she needed watching, and she needed someone to do for her the things of the world, like washing and dressing, because she had little use for them herself. My sister could not manage this on top of keeping the things of the farm running, and we had to whittle down those who could help.

My other sister and brother had obligations to return to. My younger sister had children, and her life lay there, so we all agreed she would have to go back as soon as the weekend was over. My brother had work in times when few did, and he was not a wealthy man, so had to keep it. His work was in the town and he had no choice but to live there. He could come up at weekends, though his wife would be reluctant to let him go every week.

My brother and sisters, I realised, knew very little about my life or the work I did. They knew I had been the clever one but because, on the island, intelligence was only considered valid if it led to success in the boxed world, no-one really discussed what I did as an architect because they did not quite trust it, and in case it transpired that it should be less than respectable in some way.

Sitting around the kitchen table listening to the choices and how they would be made, I knew it would have to be me. I had worked quietly all these years, and was due at least several months' sabbatical or at least some entitlement to compassionate leave. I could take it there and work remotely, which this age allows when the people inside the structures have enough imagination. Thankfully, my immediate superiors were open to persuasion.

When I told my brother and sisters this, looks of relief shot across their faces, tinged with a speck of doubt about what it all entailed. I explained that I would have to work, of course, but could do so from here, and that I would be able to help with my mother on a daily basis. And that was how I began the long wait alongside my sister, and how I came to discover where my mother had gone.

* * * * * * *

The initial few months were not easy. My sister and I crossed frequently in mild frustration when my need to work was overruled by more pressing matters with my mother or on the farm. I have noticed that anyone working at home is not given as much credibility or space as someone confined to an office. Maybe it is the fact that when you leave in the morning for the office, everyone respects your space and is mildly afraid to encroach upon it. Maybe its rationale lies in the fact that offices involve visible superiors, and are situated safely in an area out of bounds to the general public, so family members do not generally phone or arrive for cups of tea. Or maybe it is because people just take advantage where they can in their own efforts to offload what they cannot cope with themselves, and they do not give enough thought to how it is offloaded.

Whatever the cause, when you work from your home, you are in danger of people interrupting the whole day with trivialities which seem more important to them than if you were safely confined behind office bars. On the whole, though, my sister and I established a routine where I worked in the mornings and was considered "out somewhere on the farm" if anyone called wondering where I was. In the afternoons I did whatever was required, and that was that.

It soon became clear, though, that my mother was not coming back to us in the near future. We were beginning to wonder if we had made the right decision, and at times my sister and I became agitated with one another, because we were living with doubts. When the initial period of my leave was over, I had to return to the city to renegotiate things. I knew I would not be able to go back to the world of boxes as I had come to depend on it. For some reason, it was receding even as I tried to negotiate an extension to my leave.

My only real choice was to call on a few contacts and set up as a consultant, which would allow me to come and go. It would not solve all my sister's problems, but at least I could work from her house on the island most of the time, and there would be no long-term repercussions. I had no idea how long the wait would last.

My mother went about her business. The smile never left her face, at least when we were watching her, and she never seemed the worse for anything. We did have to watch carefully, though. On occasions, especially at dusk in the moments before the sun set, she sometimes tried to walk away. We could never be sure if she was heading for the cliffs, or where she might end up, so at first we brought her back. After a while, though, we followed her, to see where she was trying to go. Usually it was nowhere, or so it seemed, and she came back of her own accord.

Of all of us, I was the most curious about where my mother went – not on her walks around the island, but the place her eyes went when they stared out over the sea. I watched her more and more for clues, but she remained behind her curtain and I could not enter, no matter how much I wanted to understand.

As the time wore on, I became more and more used to the place I had been forced to return to. I was a curiosity to our neighbours, who had never quite known what to make of me, and I was hardly the life and soul of the community, but they did eventually stop speculating openly about me, and left me to my own devices. I, on the other hand, eventually began to tire of the tedium and lack of stimulation. I started to accompany my mother on her walks, and she did not seem to mind my company. She was going, whether I went with her or not.

We walked in silence and in the shadows, because my mother had not uttered a word since the start of her confinement. She did not seem to need the words, and by walking with her in silence, I found a way to climb in there with her, just as I used to do as a child when I was afraid. I did not need to understand where I was going, because I trusted her not to lead me into any harm.

One evening, we walked further than usual and arrived at the other side of the island where the tower was. Because I had grown up with it and taken it for granted, I had never really thought of the tower as a folly. I only became interested in those later, and assumed they were a thing of the expansive estates in the mainland. But a folly it was, sitting there incongruously on the hill, and all alone. It was a ruin, but always had been, and was built that way. It awakened my interest, and I returned there the following day without my mother.

The tower was built of irregular stone, and tilted the wrong way on the edge of an incline, sitting, it almost seemed, on thin ice. It had been the brainchild of a landowner who had wanted somewhere to view the stars, and who had a love of the absurd and the lop-sided. He had built a place where the earth met the sky in glorious limbo, and which had the appearance of having been erected upside down. No-one locally took it seriously. Its edges spilled out over the hillside and straggled down them as though they were reluctant to stop. It had once had several storeys and a winding staircase, and a drawbridge made of wood which operated on a pulley system and afforded the landowner the luxury of hiding himself away inside. All these things were long gone, rotted away by the damp and the neglect, and all that remained were the stone walls. Remarkably it still stood, and was more robust than the house it had once accompanied in this isolated part of nowhere.

I had taken a flask of strong coffee, one of the few vices I allowed myself these days, as it had the satisfying habit of revitalising my tired imagination. I sat down on one of the tower's straggling walls and drank some to warm myself up in the bitter wind. It was early autumn, which came with its changeable winds blowing out of nowhere, bouncing off the walls of our houses with explosive venom. I contemplated the landscape the tower encompassed, and realised for the first time that I was living in an uncharacteristic no man's land where I had no structure or direction to my life. I found myself sitting in an odd space between points on the compass, and never in my life had I been at such a crossroads.

The warmth of the coffee focused my imagination and I felt something crunch beneath my feet. Without bringing my thoughts back to ground, I bent down to pick it up. It was a small piece of beach-worn coloured glass of the kind you don't find any more since the authorities have taken to cleaning up all the jetsam and sanitising the planet. I dug my heels into the shale and gravel I was standing on, and realised there were more of the pieces of frosty glass, misshapen and twisted, of all sizes. I scrambled amongst it, trying not to cut myself, because in a layer below, the pieces became sharper and some had stained glass patterns on them. They were so small the patterns had long ago broken up into chaos.

In fact, there seemed to be no end to them. A great heap in proportions that could not have been there by accident. Someone had once collected the pieces over a long period of time and gathered them all in this dung pile of vitreous waste and covered it over with time and earth.

I was not a collector. In fact, my predilection for constant movement did not allow it, as I had long ago realised that nomadic feet cannot stand still without dying. Collections are the antithesis to movement, and would have held me back, so I did not collect. On the other hand, looking down at this heap of burnt colour, I was seized by the need to build an indeterminate something from it. I justified it in my guilty subconscious by believing I was not, in fact, defiling anything at all, but saving it from the sterility of a museum store cupboard where it might have sat forever with the bones of time so that it could be owned.

I drove back to the house and picked up as many cardboard boxes as I could find lying around. I was aware that I might arouse suspicion by returning right away, because, even if I thought I was alone, there were always eyes in every corner of the island. So I waited until nightfall, and made my excuses. I took my car as far as the end of the main road and turned off the lights. It was a short walk to the tower, and carrying the boxes back full of glass would be a long chore, but I was already driven by something I thought I had lost long ago.

One by one, I filled boxes from the pit of coloured glass pieces, and I transported them back to my car until it was overflowing with them. I could not stop. There was only a small scattering left on the bottom of the pit when I closed it up with my feet, and I set off back to the house with the boxes. Anyone seeing my car would assume I was driving around in respite from the long wait for my mother to return. It was not within anyone's realm of comprehension that there might be any pleasure in it.

When I finally slept, with less night to dream, I found myself in a place where the tower had been, and instead of a structure going upwards a tunnel spun down into the hill. I was able to walk down into it, because it had rough stairs hewn into the rock and the sand, and I had to be careful they did not crumble if I put my foot too near the outer edge of them. As I proceeded into the hill, I found myself in a cellar, or cave, or something which, by nature, was underground. Hanging from the walls and on the round upper surface which served as a ceiling, were pieces of crystal on long lengths of clear sinew, like very fine glass rope. They did not move, but the light moved across them, though I could not ascertain where the light was coming from as I was inside the earth.

As I went to touch one of the pieces, to see if it was sharp or smooth, to see if it held fast on its glass string, I was jolted awake by my sister's voice calling breakfast. I did not, at first, come back from the land of the underground, nor did I wish to, but the call was angry and drew me away. I had not, apparently, responded the first three times she had called.

It was a Sunday, a day we normally moved slowly, and it was already late. Our day revolved around my mother, but on Sundays we sat a while at the kitchen table, my mother seated in the armchair by the stove. This morning I had no desire to sit and discuss the island, what it was doing and not doing, which people had horns this week and which were saints. I rummaged around in my head for excuses to stay in my room and take a look at the boxes of glass.

It was afternoon before I returned to them. My sister found a mountain of things to talk about, and somehow I could not get away. After lunch, when we had cleared up, I took advantage of the lull and slid away, but I was tired when I reached the boxes and my mind was no longer on it. I found myself half-heartedly rummaging through them, and eventually fell asleep.

I have found that, when I am especially deprived of sleep for any reason, my dreams are all the more vivid and I am so deeply entrenched in them that I cannot easily wake up. Going back to sleep is much easier, and only something obligatory wrenches me back to the world. I dreamed of the tower again, but this time, when I went in, I first encountered a large entrance hall, much bigger than the tower seemed from the outside. In it was a broad stone fireplace with a roaring fire and, it seemed to me, a long memory. It held secrets and was about to tell me them.

First, though, I found myself drawn to a staircase to the right of the fire. It spiralled upwards and upwards, passing on its way small alcoves with windows and stone benches where people could sit to peer outside. So, for a while, I did so, as I was in no hurry and was curious. I sat first at a window through which I could see a landscape which was not my own, but which made me feel the kind of warmth the sun gives out when it wraps itself around you in Spain and Portugal.

Around the tower were wild gardens with over-grown bay trees, tall as poplars, and stunted oaks and burnt grass. There was bright sunshine, so that the garden produced its own shadows, and the games it played with them were all the more visible.

In the garden were ruins, broken columns of long marble, only just apparent in the under-growth, and split by lavender and wild thyme. At intervals, a path emerged amongst the tangled, dry grass, and walked for a while before it disap-peared again from view, and along the paths were occasional stone benches for resting. Further out, beyond the tall stone walls of the garden, the landscape faded into yellow broom and low brush, and paths led away into the hills. One path became a long dusty road leading into the dis-tance and ending at an old mill, a large stone edi-fice which had a broken roof but which was smiling.

I moved on up the staircase and found myself at the next alcove, looking down through the window at a graveyard, the type found in south-ern Europe where bodies are stored in little boxes piled on top of one another. Each box has a picture of the life it once contained, and the souls sit outside in the sun to rest. Moving thinly around the spaces between the graves were wisps of coloured light, slow and graceful, like an aurora. They came and went and spoke to one another along the way.

I followed the staircase to the next alcove and this time saw an elongated oval garden, sunk into the rock to form a sort of grotto. It was approached through a small wooden gate which led down a set of steps carved out of the hillside, and into an auditorium filled with overgrown rose bushes and fallen leaves which had not been cleared for some time. It was lined with long marble seats in the Roman style, which gave onto a cavity where, I assumed, there had once been a pond. At the far end of the grotto, just beyond the auditorium, was a small shrine, which I realised was dedicated to Santa Rita, as it was littered with lost causes. As though I were in fact sitting there, rather than watching from a distance, I could hear music, a soft, low cornet playing part baroque, part something else, and it was warm in the afternoon sun.

All the windows which overlooked the gardens were minuscule, but I could see through most of them a vast panorama, and curiously, when I returned to a part I thought I had already seen, it had changed shape or migrated into a slightly different form, as though it were part of a kaleidoscope. I eventually reached the top of the tower and emerged onto a flat roof bordered by a turreted wall. The inside surfaces of the turrets were covered with a brilliant mosaic of coloured glass, not images, but patterns, each one different.

I tried to fix the patterns in my head, thinking I must remember them, but when I moved from one to the next, and then back to the last one, they had always changed. Either the light or the shapes had shifted, and not even a thin line of vision could hold them in place. I leaned over one of the turrets and was mildly surprised to notice that, instead of the sea or the moor of the island, I could see warm grasslands covered in low trees in no particular order, and dried grass which stuck up in wisps and made shadows on the ground but did not move. I tried to locate the wild gardens and the cemetery I had seen through the small windows, but could not. Whether they were hidden from this angle so high up, or whether they simply looked different from there, I could not tell. I could not even find the dusty road with the smiling mill.

Instead, I saw a river which cut a path between two dark mountains, where the shadows moved faster than I would have expected. The watercourse was a sliver in the sunlight, and wound round the mountains and back again. On the other side of the tower was a long plain with a carpet of broom and a low breeze though I am not sure how I knew. Along the plain, a road wound over the horizon and took my eyes with it until it vanished over the hill, and then I traced myself back along the road to its source at a tiny white building.

Inadvertently, I found myself reaching out to touch the glass mosaic on the stone turrets. For some reason, my fingers would not reach, and I realised it was time to leave. I set off down the winding staircase, but emerged by what seemed to be a back door, not the huge entrance hall where I had begun, and I was a little sad that the fire had told me nothing.

I turned and tried to go back into the tower, but the door had closed behind me and I felt like Alice. Something told me I could not go back in. Remarkably, I could now hear the sea, but could not see it, and began walking in panic towards the sound. Something began shaking me, and I was jolted out of my dream back into the bedroom. My sister had become alarmed at my absence and, not being able to rouse me even by shouting and shaking me, had called the doctor.

My heart sank. She had, without doubt, set in motion a string of bureaucracy which would involve me in endless days in the town taking tests for the same things that had baffled them about my mother. I tried to tell them there was nothing to be alarmed about, but my behaviour did not fit any of the anticipated boxes and so would need to be investigated until it did. Thankfully, in the general panic, no-one seemed to have noticed all the containers lining one side of the room, and I was anxious to get them out of there before they did. I leapt out of bed with uncharacteristic agility, ushered them to the door, and said I would be down as soon as I had dressed. We could discuss all this in the kitchen.

By the time we had taken all the usual readings, blood-pressure etc., my patience was once again waning, and I asked to be excused as I had work to catch up on. I generally had the impression that my work was taken less than seriously by everyone, as it always took place in my room, and no-one ever saw the results. Besides, there was no evidence of it in the island, and clearly it was regarded as fictitious and to be interrupted as required. I regretted my choice of excuse as soon as I had said it because, predictably, the reply was, "Oh, I don't think you need to be worrying about that just now. Get some rest. Get out and see people. It'll do you good to be in company."

They were judging me by their own weaknesses. I found company stressful, especially when it was wheeled out as a cure-all. I had never understood why the health services assumed that people under stress needed company or that anything communal was even slightly relaxing. I had watched with horror as old age pensioners, perfectly happy with their knitting and television were ushered out onto bus trips to places that looked exactly like the ones they lived in, and were told it would be good for them to get out. They invariably returned battered and worn-looking from a day squeezed in amongst people with whom they had nothing in common but their age.

It is, I suppose, my own fault for not being a person given to rollicking parties. I had had to sit through too many of them as a child, where everyone was supposed to turn up so you could be seen to be there, but no-one actually liked each other very much. When it comes to clubs, I agree wholeheartedly with Groucho Marx. I had come to the conclusion long ago that the "let's get them all together" syndrome was a social rule to be resisted wherever possible, but I also knew that any protest on my part would only be used as evidence that I was unwell. We solitaries are generally considered to live within the precarious realms of mental illness.

On this occasion, I could justify it to myself without difficulty. I preferred to be left alone to investigate my boxes of glass, but it would clearly have to wait until everyone had gone to bed. And thus began the nocturnal project which unintentionally brought my mother home, for better or worse.

My mind worked in strange ways, or perhaps I was just becoming bored with the monotony of the island. On the other hand, perhaps I had indeed developed a mental illness as the doctor clearly believed, and was hurtling off down the road to "inappropriate behaviour". I had taken it into my head that I should build a tower, the folly of all follies, which would be a place for souls to reside as a respite from the angular world.

It was not easy to do it out of sight. Eyes are everywhere on an island, so it took a couple of nights of wandering around our small fields to locate a suitable position. I decided on a secluded spot where no-one was likely to go, a place on the far reaches of our land, but just far enough within it for none of our neighbours to stumble upon it. It was not that I did not want anyone to see it. I just wanted to finish it first, and then at least it would be done before anyone could stop it happening. On the other hand, I would have been just as happy to keep it a secret for ever. Secrets were much more powerful while they were kept hidden. Besides, no-one would have taken it seriously unless they could have turned it into some sort of visitable joke.

The place I chose was one I knew well as a child. It was dangerous, and I had not been allowed there on my own, but I had gone often, when no-one knew. It was even beyond the small lake, and for most people that was far enough. Past the lake where the two pairs of divers nested year after year, and where the long vein of quartz shone in the sun after it had been raining and looked like white gold, and past the hill where you could hear water trickling beneath the rocks.

There was a small stream there, and if you took time to look, hundreds of pieces of broken stone tools lay under the shallow current. Maybe they were very old, and maybe they were not, but thankfully they were not on the archaeological routes, so the authorities let them be. The stones were partly shaped by human hands, for something to plough the fields with, and partly by the water in the stream, and they were heavy with life when you held them in your palm. I always put them back, not because of any ethical consideration, but because that is where they lay. I could not bear the thought of them being taken as trophies or toys, or not being given their own space in the world.

Beyond the stream was a headland which launched itself into the ocean as though it were sailing off a ski-jump. It was dark green with shallow grass and, until you reached its edge, it seemed it would make a sheer drop into the sea like the cliffs around it. Coming closer though, it sank gently down to the shoreline in layers of uneven rock, forming shelves and pools with flora between. It depended on the tides, and waxed and waned with them, but on cold days I found shelter there from the north wind, and on warm afternoons I could sit down to rest in the sun.

On the edge of the headland were old stone walls and crevices which helped to hide it from distant eyes, and this is where I chose to build my tower. It was a good distance to walk at nights, but I knew the place like the back of my hand. You do not usually forget what you learn in your youth, no matter how far away you live from it. There was plenty of stone, scattered or built there by centuries of hands and reused and turned as it was required. I worked in the fine tradition of the wall thieves who rebuilt with whatever stone they could find in ages where the planners did not exist to wag their long fingers.

Before I started building, I set aside my usual work, took a thin pencil, and began to design my tower. It was a mesh of asymmetrical pillars and tilting stonework, hard to achieve with the sharp stone from the old field walls, but not impossible. The building was neither round nor square, but somewhere in between, and it leaned a little, as though the wind were blowing it over. It had an uneven set of turrets on the top, with a slightly sloping roof floor to let the water drain away, but still allowing a surface to stand on so that I could watch the sea on a calm day.

I drew only the shell of the tower because its crowning glory could not be drawn, and would have to wait to be brought to light. Inside, it had two storeys, each with small, thin slits for windows which framed the sea like a long needle. Alongside each window was a stone seat, for watching. But here I became impatient with the details and began, instead, to build.

I took to sleeping during the day when everyone thought I was working. I purposely missed every appointment made for me at the hospital by telling my sister the wrong date, and eventually they stopped trying. I had to wait until everyone was sound asleep before I went out, and I always returned before breakfast, as though I had just got up.

The walk to the headland was slow, but I came to look forward to it because I was enclosed only by my own thoughts, and out there in the darkness I did not have to worry that anyone would intrude on them. I began to pile up stones from the old field walls on the headland, and slowly built the base, and then the walls of the tower.

It was a tilting structure, balanced precariously and lurching towards the sea, straggling away towards the edge of the land as though it were curious about what was on the other side. It had narrow slit windows, set unevenly up through its height, and on top, what appeared to be a small cupola within the sloping roof was, in fact, an illusion. It was a convex wall which did not quite reach to its full extent, so that it did not meet in the middle. From the ground, and even from a considerable distance, it resembled a cupola. From inside it, you could stand and survey the landscape in all directions, across the sea or back over the moor. By moonlight you could watch the shapes in the land changing, even though nothing moved, though the sea welled. When the moon went behind a cloud for an instant, you could swear the waves were frozen in a frame, like a film stuck on the reel, and then they emerged again, no further on in their journey.

The staircase had had to be made of stone too, so was a crude tower in itself, a little rickety and unstable but not high, so if I was careful I knew I would not fall far. Inside the walls I had placed lintels at intervals, elongated tear-shaped stones which were lying around everywhere in the old field walls and had perhaps once held up the door to a building. They helped stabilise the tower's walls, but also allowed me to toy with patterns, mosaics of the rough stone, varying the wall's monotony.

Then came the night when I began to carry over the glass. I carried a box at a time in a wheelbarrow and made heavy work of it because I was impatient, and this was an unnecessary delay. Before I could transport all the boxes out there, however, something happened to delay the plans further. The doctor, clearly frustrated by my deliberate attempts to evade her, announced she was going to the town and would be happy to take me down for those tests. Had this not been said in front of my sister, I would have made multiple excuses about pressing work, and would have found a way out. But my sister was delighted with the idea and accepted on my behalf. My sister always took opportunities because they did not happen often.

I endured the long journey to the town, trying hard to make conversation with someone who, I realised, had a jaded view of the world and was determined everyone would share it. At first I tried hard to say innocuous things about the weather or the seasons, which could not provoke any dissent, but it became apparent that whatever I said would be taken to mean something else. So after a while I sat in silence, and was relieved when we reached the hospital.

Our doctor clearly did not trust me, so accompanied me to the appropriate waiting area until she was forced to leave to attend to whatever had brought her to the town. I resigned myself to my fate, and adopted a waiting mode where I found some mild amusement in watching the people come and go into the consultant's room in no apparent order.

I was finally admitted to the inner sanctum and asked a variety of questions which were answered by a series of tick-boxes on the man's desk. He was surly, as important doctors often are, and had a tendency to peer at me over his rather old-fashioned glasses. He did not seem much like a person who would resort to tick boxes, but then again, he had no doubt long ago been commandeered by the system, and he had the appearance of being mildly bored.

At length, he stood up, shook my hand, placed in it a sheet of paper with scribbles on it, and directed me down a corridor. "There is nothing wrong with you," he said, "but I'm afraid that diagnosis may not be what everyone wants to hear, so you may have to bear with me while I send you through the motions. It shouldn't take too long, and then you'll be free to go."

I smiled at him, though he did not smile back. He only looked at me wearily as though all this were happening at my own request, and he showed me the door. I realised he was a man of some considerable imagination who had been locked into a similar life to my own, and could not get out. Perhaps he had once been allowed to cure people in his own way, who knows.

I proceeded down a long corridor where I was met by a desk. Behind the desk sat a woman in a white uniform who did not look up from her paperwork. At intervals, she got up from her desk and took a piece of paper through one of the doorways bordering the room, but did not acknowledge my presence in any way. I stood there for some time, perhaps five minutes, before I wondered if I should say anything, but the atmosphere did not lend itself to enquiries. I left my piece of paper on her desk and sat down in a corner by some magazines.

When I looked up a few minutes later, my piece of paper had disappeared from the desk and was undergoing some form of processing by the lady in the white coat, who still did not show any signs of acknowledging my presence. After half an hour I plucked up enough courage to ask if I was in the right place. She looked up from her paperwork and asked where my note was from the consultant. When I looked bewildered, she said, "Did the doctor not give you a piece of paper to bring down here?"

I told her I had left it on her desk and had seen her take it somewhere with a pile of other papers. "Oh," she replied without a smile. "You should have given it to me. Now I don't know which doctor it's gone to and I'll have to go and look for it. Next time, you have to give it to me."

I sincerely hoped there would be no next time, and sat back in my seat, having been given a severe ticking off and thankful no-one else was in the room. I have never been given to reading magazines in waiting rooms as they always seem to be uninteresting. On this occasion, though, I picked one up absentmindedly in an attempt to do what I thought might be expected of me, hoping this would improve my ultimate chances of a favourable diagnosis.

In fact, it turned out to be a publication featuring an article on mediaeval castles in Portugal, so it took my attention at once. At this point, however, just as I was beginning to get into the stride of the long wait, I was wrenched away by the sharp sound of my name and called down another corridor, where I underwent a series of tests and was then told I was free to go.

I ignored my better judgement and set off for the bus station, hoping the doctor would find her own way home and realise I had left without her. I would have to deal with that later. On my arrival at the bus station, however, I was greeted by a police siren and a man in uniform running towards me. He had apparently been alerted by our vigilant doctor that a patient had absconded and could be about to do himself some damage. I resigned myself to my fate, as this had already gone too far and was out of my hands. An afternoon of paperwork cleared the matter up, but I was forced to endure icy company on the journey home.

My sister, to her credit, closed the incident off with a laugh and promised she would not force me down that route again. We had become closer through it all, I think, through having to be. She was a good person, just a little jaded by the small world, and when she needed to, she could see outside of it.

My world was disjointed after breaking the pattern of sleep and sleeplessness that I had invented for myself, and I was unnerved. I dozed in an acquiescent way to try and rid myself of the intrusions of humanity, and awoke at three in the morning, too late to venture out to the tower and too early to get up and join the daily world. I began assembling the tiny pieces of glass into small mosaics, conjunctions of colour and focus which seemed to draw themselves and follow one another without my intervention.

The shades were unusual, faded yellows and oranges on green and red, here and there a blue which resembled more the mineral or plant extract it had come from, and which modern dyes cannot even approach. They sometimes had the appearance of sand, not in hue, but in texture, and the reds were especially grainy, as though they had soaked up the dye out of hunger.

The patterns formed and grew, and I collected them onto boards, to be joined together later in the walls of the tower. I resumed my work each night, re-finding the rhythm I had lost after the hospital incident, and the closer I came to finishing the work, the more anxious I was that it should not be discovered before it could be finished.

When the mosaics were completed, I took them two at a time out to the headland, and, as best I could without falling towards the sea, carefully cemented them to the outside walls of the tower. The waves were never silent, but threatened sometimes more than others, and I learned to live with them again as I had done as a child.

I always had to go home before dawn, a frustration because I was not ready to return, but anything short of that would endanger the whole project. When it was finished, though, I allowed myself to go back during the day to see the glass glinting in the sun. If it had been raining, it shone more brightly than any lighthouse, and ships must surely have seen it, and said nothing.

Only when I was satisfied that the structure was completely ready, both inside and out, did I rest, and my mind cleared enough for me to understand what I had to do next. That night, I awoke my mother from her sleep, which was light because she rarely left it completely, and led her by the hand across the moor to the headland. She did not resist, as I suspect she either knew, or did not care, where we were going.

When we reached the tower, I gently edged her inside, intending to follow, but the doorway was narrow and we could not both enter together. Once inside the tower, her hand slipped from mine, and I was forced to let it go. Instead, I followed her into the small round hallway I had created just inside the structure, but could not find her. My hand reached for the stairway, to feel for signs of her there, but there was nothing. Somewhere along the journey my mother had vanished into wherever it was she went, but this time I could not even see her, and I feared she may have gone from our world forever.

I felt my way up the staircase and emerged onto the roof of the tower within the light of the small moon. A breeze was blowing up, and I stood for a long time watching the waves and not caring where my mother was or where she was going. If she wished, she would – I assumed – return of her own accord, and in the meantime I watched the edges of the waves as they emerged into the moonlight and faded again.

I have no idea how long I stood there, but gradually I became aware of the waves gathering pace and the breeze strengthening. Island winds have a mind and a soul of their own, and do not follow men's rules. They defy science and prediction, and they sneak up if you turn your back even for an instant. They demand respect, and do not take kindly to bravado or flippancy.

The breeze, without much warning as I remember, became a gale and wound itself into a frenzy. It cannot have taken long, because I did not notice its passage until it was nearly at full force, and I found myself holding tightly to the sides of the tower to avoid being swept away by the sudden gusts. I struggled down the staircase, back into the base of the tower, aware that I should find my mother before the weather became any worse. She could not have gone far in the dark, but on the other hand I was aware how well she knew these shores and what little regard she had for our anxieties about her disappearances.

She was nowhere in or around the tower, and outside the wind was making it hard to see anything. It was blowing into my eyes, and despite the approaching dawn I could make out very little. The wind was now cracking against the sides of the tower, and weakening the structure so that rocks were coming loose from the sides and spilling out onto the ground. At first I tried to put them back, bolstering up the walls with my own strength, but the mosaic glass was also coming loose and my fingers were catching on its sharp edges. I became aware that my hands were bleeding. Far from causing me any pain, however, the slime was simply a nuisance, and was preventing me from getting a proper grip of the stones.

At some point the wind began to explode, as it sometimes did when it was on a winning streak, and it started to take whole pieces of wall apart and dump them into the sea. The tiny pieces of glass began to break up, and went soaring over the cliff as though in slow motion, on a quiet bid for freedom. They sank into the churning of the waves and landed at the bottom of the sea, on the beach and in the air, wherever the moment threw them.

Piece by piece the whole structure of the tower collapsed and floated over the edge of the headland as though it had always been going there, and as though that were why it had existed in the first place. It had been destined for chaos because it was, in fact, chaos itself. It was quite at home in the ether.

As far as I could with the salt wind attacking my eyes, I watched it disappear and I no longer felt any pain, but instead I wept. I wept for all the people who, like me, had tried and failed. I sat down on the ground to steady myself while I watched, and after a while I began to walk slowly over the moor to our house, wondering how I would explain to my sister that we had finally lost my mother and that I was to blame.

Strangely for the circumstances, I did not feel guilt, but relief, even though I anticipated the consequences. I had broken the rules of what most people saw as common sense and propriety, but I had also broken a deadlock, whatever it had been, and somehow – though I had no idea how – we could move on now, all of us. As I approached the house, though, I saw a figure standing in the doorway, and did not at first make sense of it as I should have. It was still early, and no-one else was up.

As I came closer, the figure went inside, and I could make out the shape in the kitchen window of someone going about their daily business, whether I was there or not. Someone was making tea, or breakfast, I could not see which. She was quiet and composed, and was bringing order to the room without imposing it.

As I approached the door, my mother came out onto the cobbled terrace in front of our house with a cup of tea, steaming in a mug, and offered it to me with a smile. Not an absent smile this time, but one which greeted me, and I knew we had brought her home. I also knew it would not be the last time we would lose her, nor the last time we would find her again. She was one of the lucky ones, who could come and go at will, and not one of us could hold her down.

The medical authorities were sceptical about my mother's return. Predictably, it made them uneasy and they were happy to give us the responsibility of "keeping an eye on it." My sister's relief soon gave way to the furrowed brow which told me she did not relish being left alone again in this place, but I did not allow myself to be turned.

I left for the city a little the wiser. I knew now where my mother went on her journeys, and was happy to let her go, though I knew others would not be so acquiescent. We would all too soon be there again, trying too hard to discover what she was staring at in the ether. ∎

17752759R00128

Made in the USA
Middletown, DE
06 February 2015